"Millie, do you really want to interview me tonight?" Dan asked.

The expression in his eyes should have warned her. The huskiness in his voice should have warned her. The musky scent of sexual desire should have warned her that the time had come.

Dan touched her with nothing save his eyes, those smoky, intense gray eyes, yet she felt his brand on every part of her body. In her lonely heart, in her most secret places. Wherever his gaze touched, she blazed.

"Wouldn't you rather see where this heat takes us?" he asked.

She felt rooted to the spot, powerless to deny the hunger she read in his eyes.

"Tell me that you want me as much as I want you."

She did. Shamelessly. She'd waited so long, and now she would have him at last. "Yes. . . ."

WHAT ARE *LOVESWEPT* ROMANCES?

They are stories of true romance and touching emotion. We believe those two very important ingredients are constants in our highly sensual and very believable stories in the *LOVESWEPT* line. Our goal is to give you, the reader, stories of consistently high quality that may sometimes make you laugh, sometimes make you cry, but are always fresh and creative and contain many delightful surprises within their pages.

Most romance fans read an enormous number of books. Those they truly love, they keep. Others may be traded with friends and soon forgotten. We hope that each *LOVESWEPT* romance will be a treasure—a "keeper." We will always try to publish

LOVE STORIES YOU'LL NEVER FORGET
BY AUTHORS YOU'LL ALWAYS REMEMBER

The Editors

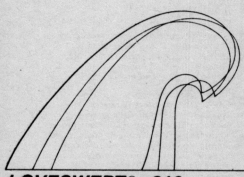

LOVESWEPT® • 316

Doris Parmett

Diamond in the Rough

 BANTAM BOOKS
TORONTO • NEW YORK • LONDON • SYDNEY • AUCKLAND

DIAMOND IN THE ROUGH
A Bantam Book / March 1989

If you would be interested in receiving protective vinyl
covers for your Loveswept books, please write to this address
for information:

Loveswept
Bantam Books
P.O. Box 985
Hicksville, NY 11802

ISBN 0-553-21968-5

Published simultaneously in the United States and Canada

Bantam Books are published by Bantam Books, a division
of Bantam Doubleday Dell Publishing Group, Inc. Its trademark, consisting of the words "Bantam Books" and the
portrayal of a rooster, is Registered in U.S. Patent and
Trademark Office and in other countries. Marca Registrada.
Bantam Books, 666 Fifth Avenue, New York, New York 10103.

PRINTED IN THE UNITED STATES OF AMERICA

O   0 9 8 7 6 5 4 3 2 1

To Isabel Helfman, the only living saint I know. Thank you, love, for more than I can possibly list.

And to Michael A. Haines, crime prevention officer of the New Providence Police Department, for patiently answering all my questions and then some.

One

It was too darn hot to play cops and robbers. The
scent of citrus from a nearby orange grove hung
heavy in the Florida air. At 8:00 A.M., the temper-
ature was eighty-five degrees and climbing.

Detective Sergeant Daniel J. Murdock was slouched
down in the seat of his unmarked police vehi-
cle, waiting for the Goldberg grocery store to open.
His seersucker jacket, worn to conceal his weapon,
made him hotter. To top it off, the car's air con-
ditioner was on the fritz.

Only Murdock's anticipation of locking up Louie
"The Juice" Simono made the wait palatable. Willing to do anything the mob asked, Louie led a
charmed life. For services rendered, he had received their blessing to "juice"—extort money—
from elderly store owners. As an added bonus, the
mob gained an outlet to launder money.

Dan popped two Chiclets into his mouth, wishing they were Swiss chocolate instead. Sucking the sugar coating from gum didn't rate the same sensual thrill as letting a piece of candy melt in his mouth, but it would have to do. He'd lost five pounds in one week. He intended to shed another three; then he'd be back at his fighting weight. One hundred eighty-five pounds of muscle—if he didn't count the slight pinch of skin at his waistline. Not bad for an old man of thirty-six.

Without thinking, he reached into the inside pocket of his jacket. Yielding to another one of life's pleasures, he lit an unfiltered cigarette, filled his lungs with two deep drags, and broke out in a fit of coughing. He wiped the tears from his eyes and waited for the burning sensation in his chest to clear. He hadn't smoked in a month.

"Damn," he mumbled, crushing the cigarette in the ashtray. "Nothing's fun anymore."

He glanced toward the store. He couldn't see anyone, but he knew that the Goldbergs were inside, along with his partner, Ben Jackman. Ben was wearing a wire so they could tape everything Louie said. Thirty-four years old, Ben was a tall, redheaded Irishman, and the freckles on his face added to his boyish charm. He and Dan had been partners for years.

Even before he heard the automobile's tires making the turn into the lot, Dan's finely tuned reflexes warned him of an approaching car. *Louie.* He welcomed the surge of adrenaline in his veins, the rush that would carry him through.

He glanced in the side view mirror, already imagining collaring Louie. But . . . "What the hell!"

Louie didn't drive a red convertible with the top down. And by no stretch of the imagination did he resemble the attractive, dark-haired woman behind the wheel.

He wasn't about to let her screw up his operation. Louie's early morning visits were understandable. He arrived an hour before the stores opened because he didn't want witnesses. What was *she* doing here?

Parking right in front of the Goldberg grocery, that's what!

Dan yanked the mike off its clip under the dashboard. He read off her license-plate number to the dispatcher, then waited for the computer to run a check on the plates. Dan knew everything was in the timing, and he swiveled to keep the woman in his line of vision.

He groaned. His hopes for a nice, uncomplicated arrest sank as she made no move to get out of her car. Instead, she produced a hairbrush and began to brush her thick mane of hair.

Under other circumstances he'd study her elegant profile—her straight nose, her high cheekbones, the sweeping line of her jaw, and, from the tilt of her chin, her equally elegant neck. When he was on stakeout for long, tedious hours and he spotted an attractive woman, he'd usually let himself daydream. It helped kill the boredom. Sometimes he'd fill in the blanks, harmlessly providing her with a whole family history—if she had what it took to interest him.

The woman turned her head, giving him his first opportunity to see her face clearly. *Stunning.*

The word rushed into his mind. Almond-shaped blue eyes, a stubborn chin, and cheekbones a model would envy. She tossed the cloud of chestnut hair over her bare shoulders. Individual strands of nutmeg and amber caught the sunlight, an iridescent symphony.

She definitely had what it took to interest him—but not now. Now he just wanted her out of there.

With a growing sense of desperation, Murdock saw her lean her head back on the red leather headrest and close her eyes. "Lady," he muttered, "be a good girl and scram."

He alternated between checking the seconds ticking by and cursing, then decided to take matters into his own hands. His one overriding concern was to get her out of harm's way. He got on the microphone again and spoke hurriedly to Ben. "There's a civilian parked in front of Goldberg's. I'm going to go to her." Then he issued orders to the officers waiting off the lot in unmarked patrol cars.

"All units, there's a woman in the line of fire. After Louie comes out, make the arrest at the end of the parking lot. Repeat, the end of the lot. We don't want to give the Goldbergs a heart attack or involve the civilian." His command reconfirmed, Dan sprinted out of his car.

He had exactly three minutes.

Millie Gordon sighed with contentment as the warm sun bathed her face. It didn't bother her that Goldberg's wasn't open yet. She'd wait. When she'd gotten up that morning, she hadn't been certain what to do—go to the beach; peck away at her computer as her alter ego, the syndicated advice columnist, *Ask Ms. M*; or, finally, get back to her book, *Not-Your-Run-of-the-Mill People*, a collection of in-depth interviews of unusual people in exciting occupations. The beach won. It was a lovely day, and she meant to enjoy it to the fullest.

"I'm fresh out of intelligent advice and I can't find the energy to work on the book," she'd confided to her agent, Wylie McGuiness, on the phone the day before. "I've roughed out that chapter on the concert pianist, but I'm just not interested in it."

"Take a breather, Millie," Wylie had advised in her thick Brooklynese. "What good is vacationing in Florida if you don't take time to smell the roses? Go work on your tan. It should look great with your blue eyes. Better yet, find a man and let him tell you you look great."

"The trouble with you, Wylie, is that you think marrying one man after another until you get it right is the solution to everything. I've come to terms with my widowhood. I've had my shot at happiness. Stop worrying about me. I'll be all right. You know you can't keep this girl down."

"That's what I like about you, Millie. You're so positive. Then get back to the book next week. I got an extension on the due date from the publisher, but remember, you've got to make this new deadline."

Millie wasn't sure the timing was right. Yawning into the phone, she had promised to get off her duff. Make some progress. Write.

That was last night.

Today, she'd awakened feeling marvelous, like her old self. Unfortunately, work was the furthest thing from her mind.

She sighed again, anticipating a long, lazy day on . . .

The passenger door of her car was yanked open. She was more startled than frightened as a man dropped onto the seat next to her.

"Lady"—a shiny badge swept past her nose—"don't be scared . . . Detective Sergeant Dan Murdock of the Port Rico Police Department. I want you to come with me. If you don't your life could be in danger. Hurry up, we haven't much time."

Millie glanced around the peaceful lot, then turned back to the man. Nuts, pretenders, and loonies came in all sizes and shapes. Her files were filled with letters proving the world was populated by strange people. Some sent pictures. Some were even handsome—like the man whose gaze was now fixed steadily on hers. She caught a trace of cigarette smoke clinging to him.

For a moment she was tempted to tell him to go take a flying leap for charging into her car unannounced. She'd never been one to scare easily. If this total stranger expected her to leave her car and trot after him like some obedient puppy on this flimsy pretense, he had another guess coming.

"Much time for what?" she asked, stalling, while her brain feverishly sorted out her options.

Apparently her slow reaction time irritated him.

He pointed to his wristwatch. "Lady, just get out of the car and come with me. Trust me."

"Why should I?"

He looked taken aback, as though this were the first time anyone had dared challenge him. The badge flew under her nose again. Annoyed, she shoved his hand away, then reached into her bag. She came up with a can of hair spray and aimed it.

"Hold it, buster. Shove that little tin badge in my face one more time and your eyelashes will have a permanent curl. Now suppose you tell me what this is all about?"

He leaned closer and precisely enunciated every syllable. "You're interfering with police business." In one swift motion he grabbed the can of hair spray. For a moment they simply stared at each other, gauging opposing wills, neither acknowledging that he'd lifted her "weapon" as easily as one takes candy from a baby. "I'm not required to give you chapter and verse," he went on. "Just do as I say. I'd hate to have to drag you out of here."

With a firm set of her lips, she dared him to try. If what he said were true, surely she'd have noticed some police activity. But the streets were calm. All she heard was peaceful silence. As if to verify her thoughts, a flock of birds flew gracefully overhead. Adding up all this tranquility, she didn't believe a word the man said. Unless . . . Of course! She should have realized the game he was playing right away.

"You're from that new television show, aren't you?" she asked. "The one with the dumb name,

Can We Fool You? Well, you can't." She had the satisfaction of seeing a red flush creep up the man's neck. He started to say something, but she rushed on. "I've always been good at spotting phonies, mister, whoever you really are. The whole idea for the program is dumb. You may tell *that* to your producer. Give the money you'd pay me to charity. And take my advice. The next time you concoct a preposterous story, make sure you have the proper setting. Besides," she added smugly, "you couldn't scare a kitten. You're going to need a few more lessons if you want someone to believe your act."

Dan recovered his wits at about the time she stopped spouting her nonsense. He clamped his hand on her wrist, then dropped it, warned off by the stiffening of her shoulders. "Do I look like a television actor?" he demanded.

Millie considered his question, studying his tanned face for ten long seconds. He was good-looking enough to be an actor. In fact, he was so handsome, he could play a leading role. His gray eyes, rimmed in black lashes, reminded her of a turbulent sea before a storm. His nose was slightly misaligned, giving him a certain toughness. Black hair, liberally sprinkled with gray at the temples, curled impudently at his nape. She wasn't afraid of him. If he were going to hurt her, he'd have done so by now.

"How do I know what actors look like?" she asked. "Maybe you are who you claim to be. And maybe you're not." Maybe he was an escaped nut from an asylum, she thought. "In either case, I'm not stupid enough to dash off with a strange man who flashes a badge in my face and makes up an absurd story. I don't even owe money on a parking ticket. You are looking at a sterling citizen."

"What I'm looking at is a fool. Now either move this car fast, or come with me."

"That does it." She didn't care for his bossy tone. "No one, I mean no one, orders me around."

Dan glowered at her. He couldn't fault her logic. Under other circumstances, he'd commend her. "Dammit, lady, Juice Louie and Spike Harvey are expected in less than a minute."

It was those ridiculous names that convinced Millie this attractive man wasn't playing with a full deck. She rolled the silly names on her tongue. They were perfect for the movies. "Juice Louie," she said, trying to keep a straight face. "That's very nice, detective. I should have introduced myself. This week I'm Madonna."

She was treated to a hard, suspicious stare. "You don't believe me?"

A knot of irritation worked its way through the pit of her stomach. She let it out little by little. "*What I believe*," she fired back, "is that you've been reading too many Damon Runyon stories. *What I know* is that unless you get out of my car, I'm going to make a citizen's arrest."

A decidedly impolite sound came from the man's mouth.

"Mister, I neither know nor care who you really are or what your game is. Anyone can flash a little tin badge. Everyone's into labels, medals, and badges these days. Since there are no police around here, it can't be as dangerous as you claim. I'm perfectly safe." She returned his stare. She added, "I'd better be."

His hand clamped around her wrist again and stayed there. His mouth was a hard line of anger. "Why are you acting so stupid? You're no kid. A woman your age should know better. Let's go."

"*I beg your pardon!*" She might be thirty-three, she thought, but she was hardly Whistler's mother. "If you don't remove your hand from my wrist, I'm going to scream bloody murder. If you try to harm me, let me remind you it's broad daylight and this is a convertible."

Bile rose in Dan's throat. How did he get such bad luck? If she screamed, she'd spook the Goldbergs. Not to mention warning off Louie. He gave serious consideration to knocking her out, then dragging her body into the rear of the store. Thinking of the wrongful arrest charges this fiery citizen would probably bring, he cursed liberally.

"That kind of language isn't necessary," she said haughtily.

Dan disagreed. Of all the confounded, lousy dumb luck . . . Of all the women in the whole wide world who might have parked there, he had to lock horns with a gorgeous Doubting Thomas.

"Thanks to your obstinate nature, lady, we're both stuck. Now it's too late." He pointed to his watch. "In less than thirty seconds, a blue Mercedes with two goons inside will be joining us. I assure you, they'll have guns in their car.

Guns with magazine clips that repeat, just in case they didn't kill the first time. They're not big on conversation, so don't plan on talking to them and driving them crazy, too." He angled his head. "They're going to go into that store and Louie will make his weekly pickup."

Millie felt the first real stirrings of uncertainty. Still, she clung to a lingering skepticism. A woman couldn't be too sure in this day and age. "Weekly pickup for what?"

Dan frowned at her. "Money," he said sarcastically. "You didn't think I meant groceries, did you?" Now why couldn't he be talking to a nice, sensible, hysterical woman who'd run like hell at the first sign of trouble? Ten more precious seconds elapsed. It felt like ten years.

Millie's assurance wavered. "Why should I believe you? I don't see any police here. Where's your backup? Are you wearing a wire?"

He quickly flipped open his jacket, exposing his Smith and Wesson high-speed thirty-eight. "No, I'm not 'wearing a wire.' Will this do? And lady, believe me, it's no toy. The bullet enters the body, making a hole the size of a pencil point. It exits with a hole big enough to put your head in and not get your ears wet."

Millie shuddered. "You needn't be so graphic."

He ignored her comment. "Look in your rearview mirror. What do you see?"

She looked. She saw a blue Mercedes. It slowly turned into the lot. Her hand lifted to her throat. "Would you happen to know the license plate number?" she asked weakly.

Without a backward glance, Dan rattled it off.

Coming abruptly to her senses, Millie slid down in the seat. "And I wasted all this time not believing you."

"You damn near ruined everything. And don't you dare faint on me, lady."

"Millie," she said, swallowing hard. "My name's Millie Gordon. And don't worry, I never faint."

"Good." He softened his tone. "Okay, Millie. Since we can't make a run for it, you and I are going to have to convince Louie we're parked here for a reason other than shopping."

She gazed into his eyes, fighting her rising panic. Her heart beat double-time. "I'll do whatever you say."

"Anything?"

"Anything."

He was already leaning toward her, shielding her body with his, blocking out the sun, blocking out everything but himself. "Okay, sugar." He grinned. "It's show time. Pucker up."

Before she could protest, his mouth covered hers. He pressed her down onto the seat, hiding her so completely with his large frame that a passerby could see only her legs. Stunned, she began to squirm, only to have him breathe a warning about sending Louie the "wrong signal."

At first his kiss was tentative, his lips merely resting on hers. Then he began to explore her mouth. His tongue slipped between her lips, and a rocket seemed to hurtle through her. Lightning jolted along her entire nervous system. Sensations of sounds, textures, and the scent of Dan

Murdock swirled through her brain. Fear of Louie receded, replaced by something more powerful and dangerous—arousal. A year of loneliness had primed her, left her vulnerable.

Even knowing Dan's kisses were play-acting of the most serious order didn't stop her body from reacting. The danger wasn't from any crooks. The danger seemed to come from the stranger kissing her, making her tremble with desire. Embarrassed, she struggled against him.

They heard a car door slam. "Help me, Millie," Dan whispered against her lips.

His plea galvanized her into action. She looped her arms around his neck, making it look as though she couldn't get close enough to his warm body. She ran her fingers through his thick, silken hair. Her mind was filled with fear, excitement, curiosity, and the nettling worry that Dan hadn't been telling the truth after all.

Dan moved suggestively, intent on convincing Louie and Spike they'd stumbled upon two passionate people who couldn't wait until they were alone. But Millie's body, pressed beneath his, was making him forget Louie. He felt her softness, her breasts flattened against his chest. He inhaled her clean scent. Even in a situation like this, a man would have to be dead not to be aware of her.

Coarse laughter bombarded their ears. "Hey, Juice." Dan recognized Spike Harvey's voice. "Getta load of those two. It's better than the video we watched with them broads last night."

Juice chortled. "Come on, Spike. Give the guy

some privacy. Ain't you got no class? Besides, we got business."

Feeling Millie flinch, Dan tightened his arms around her. He heard the door to the grocery store swing open and immediately eased himself off her. Gazing into her eyes, he guessed he looked as stunned as she did. She'd kissed him, really kissed him. He hadn't imagined the sweetness of her mouth. In the space of a moment this woman had become important to him. Did lightning really strike that fast? he wondered.

Millie struggled to put a clamp on her rampaging emotions. Lust—unplanned, unwanted lust—had betrayed her. "Is it safe?" she murmured, avoiding Dan's eyes.

"Not yet." He didn't want to scare her more than necessary, but he couldn't have her bolting either.

"Why not?"

He smoothed the hair away from her forehead. "They'll be coming out soon. My men will make the collar once they're outside. We don't want the Goldbergs involved." Or you either, he added silently.

She appeared to be considering that while he was considering his own surprising reaction to her. What had started as a ploy to fool Louie had ended up fooling him. Completely. She made his blood race.

"Tell me, Murdock," she said, "why are you acting as though you're enjoying this?"

He ruffled her hair and answered truthfully. "Must be the company. When you're not arguing, you're one helluva woman." He kissed her quickly.

"What was that for?" She heard her voice rise. "We've lost our audience."

"Me. The others were for Louie and Spike. You taste good, Millie." He frowned suddenly. "You're not married, are you?"

She was determined to keep an emotional distance from him and wasn't about to share information about her private life. "Murdock, you pick a strange time to get social." She shifted her cramped body and felt him adjust in compensation. She glared at him. "You can at least pretend for my sake."

"Not in my nature, Millie."

"I gather," she said, beginning to relax in spite of the situation, "that you're not a man who lets grass grow under his feet."

He wrapped a lock of her hair around his finger. "Just taking advantage of an opportunity thrown my way."

She shot him a look of annoyance, amazed that she wasn't in the least bit alarmed. "I could have your badge for this."

He looked affronted. "Why, Millie. After I saved your life?"

"You haven't saved it yet."

He stopped smiling. She was right. They still had a long way to go before they were in the clear. It took only one mistake, and one had already transpired.

The door to the grocery opened. "Get ready, sugar. Act Two's about to begin."

He kissed her again, putting as much enthusiasm into it as before. But the instant Louie and Spike were back in the Mercedes, he eased off her.

"Sorry, Millie, I gotta go," he said as he heard the welcome screech of tires from the four unmarked police cars. He unsnapped his holster. "Stay down until I send someone back to tell you it's clear. I mean that. Don't go getting your cute nose where it doesn't belong. I'll see you tonight."

"Just a second, Murdock. Aren't you taking a lot for granted?"

He grinned, looking like a kid about to go to a party. "Maybe so. We'll find out later. Anyway, if you were married, you'd have told me so."

"Murdock, you're a cocky so-and-so."

He nodded and kissed her lightly. A quick glance told him his men were reading Louie and Spike their Miranda rights. He hung back a few seconds more, enjoying Millie's laughter. It had the husky, deep sound of a satisfied woman. Her cheeks were flushed; her eyes sparkled with deviltry.

She was something else, he thought, admiring her. She was propped up on her elbows, and her hair flowed over the seat. He wanted to lower her right back down and pick up where he'd left off.

"You don't know where I live," she said with a smirk.

He rattled off her address. At her dumbfounded look, he added, "I even know your bra size. And that I didn't get from running a check on your license plates." He was still chuckling as he ran off.

Millie shook her head. She'd never met a man like Dan Murdock. In a flash of inspiration, she realized she'd just met the perfect candidate for the opening chapter of her book.

Two

Millie disregarded Dan's orders. After all she'd been through, she wasn't about to miss the grande finale. Besides, her fertile brain was hatching an idea. True, it was a bit vague and in need of refinement, but the perfect person had literally fallen right on top of her. It had to be fate helping her.

Arms draped over the back of the front seat, she watched the arrest as she mentally sketched her opening paragraph. "Police Detective Daniel J. Murdock is dedicated to his job . . . to the extent that he would use his own body to protect a civilian from danger." That would be a good dramatic hook. Warming to the idea, she decided to let Wylie know about her find as soon as she returned home.

Her creative juices were flowing. She was glad.

The truth was, she'd been away from excitement and people for too long.

The scene before her was right out of a movie. Wylie would love it. Police, cameramen, and reporters swarmed everywhere. Dan Murdock was in the center of it all. A thrill rippled through her, and she brushed a hand over her flushed cheek. On second thought, she wouldn't tell Wylie everything. Some details were better kept secret.

Like her scandalous behavior. She didn't need an instant replay to visualize her body's traitorous response to Murdock. How could she—a sensible woman who made her living from advising the lovelorn, lovesick, and loveless—let a smug, self-satisfied man like Dan Murdock cause a war between her nerve endings and her brain cells?

He wasn't even her type. Actually, it was better that he wasn't her type. She'd be able to write about him in a detached, professional manner. That detached, professional manner surveyed him as he worked.

She let her gaze travel down the length of his trim body. He was tall and slim hipped, with an erect bearing and broad shoulders. He had shed his jacket, revealing his well-muscled arms. She clearly remembered those arms wrapped tightly around her. In her eyes, he became a knight in shining armor.

Some knight! she hooted, correcting herself. Hardly original. *Pucker up!* Nevertheless, she didn't doubt knight Daniel possessed an impressive bag of tricks. The chapter on him would be a winner.

Neighborhood people, curious to know the source

of the commotion, began to cause a disturbance, craning their necks and jostling one another in an effort to get closer to the activity. Dan, looking every inch in control, strode over to them. He issued a terse order that sent the bystanders scurrying to the other side of the street.

She was finally able to get a clear view of Juice Louie as the cordon of officials surrounding him parted. He was spread-eagled against the front of the Mercedes. Her bubble of nervous excitement deflated. Juice Louie didn't look very tough.

Unimpressive was a better word. A small, nondescript man with thinning sandy hair, he wore a red and white striped shirt atop stark white shorts. Pale bandy legs ended in droopy white athletic socks and black shoes. She scoffed at his unprepossessing outfit.

"Absolutely no regard for taste," she murmured, thinking Louie was an ideal candidate for caricature.

Her mouth dropped open in surprise at her first good look at Spike Harvey. His blond hair, courtesy of mousse and hair spray, resembled the Statue of Liberty's crown.

"For this, Murdock tried to scare me," she muttered, gazing in wonder at the punk reject from a grade-B movie.

She tapped her fingers on the back of the leather headrest, mentally rewriting her first sentence to give it more oomph. "I had a brush with death in Florida, thanks to Detective Daniel Murdock." So what if the only thing she'd brushed up against was Detective Murdock's body?

What was wrong with her anyway? she wondered. Why was she blowing the whole thing out of proportion? This wasn't a case of a man and a woman stealing a few kisses because they couldn't stand being apart. The only reason Dan had kissed her was that he'd needed to trick some hood. Strictly police business. Nothing more.

The fact was, she realized, it was a simple case of unused hormones. Hers. Hormones she had refused to acknowledge for months. Understanding that relieved her. But it didn't explain why Dan had said he wanted to see her again.

Unbidden, memories of the heat of his lips, the bold intimacy of his powerful body, assailed her, and her throat constricted. She remembered how he had caught her by surprise with that first, open-mouthed kiss. But most of all—most shockingly and embarrassingly—she remembered the overwhelming betrayal of her own body.

And his . . .

Face it, Millie, she reasoned, Wylie's phone call unnerved you. When a woman is a ship without a rudder, anything can happen. That was what had caused her reaction. She was a widow who missed her husband. His laughter . . . even their arguments. She missed the loving. She missed so much. . . .

Catching herself slipping into self-pity, she reminded herself not to be maudlin. Anger was a much better ally. With a determined toss of her head, she slung her net beach bag over her shoulder and stepped out onto the shimmering pavement. She sniffed the fragrant citrus-scented air, delighting in the aroma. Much as she missed working in her flower and vegetable garden at her New Jersey home, nothing could compare to the lush perfume of a citrus grove.

She was about fifteen feet from her car when a plainly vexed Dan sprinted toward her. Blocking her path, he whirled her around, thus preventing Louie from seeing her face. "Millie, dammit! Just where do you think you're going?"

"I'm going to see the Goldbergs," she explained.

He brushed his hand across his forehead. "No, you're not."

"Why not?" The action was over. What right did he have to detain her?

"I've got work to do and I can't be worrying about you, too."

She waved off his concern. "That won't be necessary, I assure you. I'm quite capable of taking care of myself."

"I doubt it."

The gleam in her eye and her thrust-out jaw warned Dan. He recognized the symptoms of a delayed reaction to danger. He'd experienced it many times. Filled with unreleased tension and energized by surges of adrenaline, her body needed release. Magnificent Millie was itching for a fight. If she couldn't get Louie, he'd have to be the substitute. She was primed and pumped, raring to go a few rounds.

He understood how she felt. He could be deadly calm, capable of facing down the most ruthless criminal, going by the book and refusing to use his fists or gun except in dire emergencies. As soon as the arrest went down and the paperwork was done, his knees would start to shake. There'd be so much unexpressed emotion in him, he would feel forced to work out in the gym. Pump iron, swim, anything, until his system returned to normal.

"The Goldbergs are giving testimony to one of my men. Then they're going home. They need to cool down from the excitement. Go to the beach and swim, Millie. The exercise will do you good."

She bristled. "What's that supposed to mean? From what I recall, it was your body on top of mine, not the other way around. You're no lightweight." The quick twinkle in his eye made her blush. She knew what he was thinking.

Dan turned her around, his hands on her shoulders. He was having a hard time not remembering her womanly curves. Tender feelings or not, though, he didn't react kindly to having his commands taken lightly, not in his present mood.

"So far," he said, "you've put both our lives in danger—"

She interrupted him. "That's ridiculous. Louie and his goofy-looking friend can't be so tough. Those twerps hardly look dangerous. They're crude-mouthed creeps who make a living by scaring the wits out of old people. For that, they deserve to be sent up for a long time. But they don't scare me." She looked at Dan with cool, calculating blue eyes. "I'm disappointed in you for trying to scare me, too. Or"—she lifted an eyebrow—"did you do that on purpose?"

Dan scanned the heavens. He wanted to shake her. How could he be interested in this woman?

She'd be a thorn in any man's side. If he had a modicum of sense, he would say good riddance before tangling with this blue-eyed vixen. "You're nuts! Tell me, Millie, what does it take to scare you?"

She pointed to the crowd of onlookers. "I stayed put. I simply chose not to keep my head down. What did I do that was so different from those people over there? All I did was watch you and your men put the muscle on those hoods. They're a bunch of pip-squeaks!" His mouth twitched. "What are you laughing at?" she asked.

At her thunderous expression, he stifled the laughter bubbling up inside him. "I'm thinking about buying you a dictionary of police terms. Either that or I'll let you hang out in the locker room with the guys for a day."

Shaking off her momentary displeasure, she realized she'd just been provided the perfect opening. "I might take you up on that, Murdock."

He raised his brow, staring at her sensual mouth. He thought of how soft she had felt beneath him, how her fragrance had spun its magic, enveloping him in her trap. How her luminous eyes belied her sassy talk. But mostly he'd never let her get within thirty yards of the locker room.

"Not on your life," he said curtly.

Millie had expected a trite comeback, a remark tossed out in good humor, not the sudden tightening of his jaw or the fierceness of his answer. "You know something, Murdock? I think you have all the fun."

His gaze locked with hers, holding them both in

conflicting memories. "You know something, Millie?" he responded. "I think we could have some fun together."

She reacted to the heated sensations rushing through her, to the tingling in her breasts, shamefully aware that she must stop playing the man-woman game with him and simply tell him she'd like to interview him.

He took her hand in his, rubbing his thumb across her palm. He smiled into her eyes. "Millie, listen; I don't want you to get the wrong idea. I told you to stay down before because between them, Louie and Spike have a long rap sheet, including a couple of unprovable murders. This extortion business is only a sideline for Louie."

A tremor raced through her. Louie might look like a reject, she thought, but he was apparently dangerous. Dan had been trying to protect her and she had reacted unwisely. "But now that you've arrested them, won't they be locked up and off the streets?"

"Let's just say I want you to keep that pretty little nose of yours out of police business. An arrest isn't a conviction." He didn't think it necessary to tell her Louie was already vowing revenge, bragging he'd be out on bail within twenty-four hours.

Millie knew she was keeping him, but her curiosity got the better of her. "Why do you call him Juice Louie?"

"Because he squeezes the juice, the life blood, out of his victims. People have been known to pay him the principal on a loan six times over and still never get out from under. Maybe we'll get lucky and Spike will flip."

"Flip?"

"Turn state's evidence for a reduced charge. The term used to be 'sing.'"

The caravan of official cars began to leave the lot. One of the men shouted to Dan. Lingering another moment, Dan leaned toward her. "You're very beautiful." She was tall and graceful, reminding him of a proud huntress. Her face, honey-tan, beckoned him to stay. "My men are waiting. I'll meet you at the beach."

"The beach is a vast place, Murdock. Millions and millions of tiny grains of sand. How good are you at finding needles in a haystack?"

He rocked back on his heels, grinning. He loved a challenge. "I don't suppose you'd consider making my life easier and telling me where you'll be parked?"

She chuckled. "Let's see how good a cop you are."

"There you go again, Millie. Where's your faith? Don't you know I always get my woman?"

With a last smile, he turned and walked away. Millie returned to her car, her heart thrumming like a wild thing. Life around Dan certainly wasn't dull, she mused. In the space of an hour, her life had been in danger . . . and she'd been kissed senseless by a dark-haired hero, who carelessly referred to her now as his woman.

Dan was thinking of his foolish slip of the tongue on the drive back to the precinct. He hadn't meant to imply or suggest that he saw Millie as "his woman." He had no intention of making that sort of commitment to any woman. He had been married briefly and young to a woman named Lana, more to get her away from her drunken, abusive father than for love.

Just out of college, he had already passed the exam for the police department and had entered law school on a double-track program. After a year of marriage, Lana had decided she wanted to attend college herself. He agreed, but had to quit law school when the demands of finding the extra money became too great. He had fully intended to complete his studies after Lana got her degree. By that time, however, the marriage was over. She found a good job, and when she fell in love and remarried, he was happy for her.

He never went back to law school. As he advanced in the police department, he decided he preferred to stick to being a detective. Since then, his life had been loose and easy. It worked for him. The stress on marriages within the police community was well documented. In many precincts throughout the country, psychiatrists were on twenty-four-hour call. No, he thought somberly, recalling the tearstained, agonized face of Grant Power's widow, it was better to travel alone in this business. Besides, he hadn't met anyone to make him reconsider his decision. Unbidden, an image of a sassy brunette with cornflower-blue eyes floated in front of his face.

But no one said a little fun on the side wasn't good for the soul.

• • •

The ocean shimmered with golden sparks on gentle indigo waves. Millie swam with long, strong strokes, pushing her body through the soft, hypnotic swells. She'd been in the water for half an hour, emptying her mind of all thought. Amazingly, her body seemed starved for exercise. Tiring at last, she flipped over onto her back, floating dreamily for a while.

Finally she headed for land, shedding the last of her stored-up energy. She dragged herself out of the water and sank onto her blanket. Closing her eyes and flinging her arms above her head, she allowed her mind to drift back over the crazy morning. One image was predominant. Dan Murdock. He was as different from her husband as night from day. Frank had been methodical. He'd had the true nature of a corporate attorney.

A stream of sand trickled onto her thigh. She flipped it away, only to feel it happening again. Kids, she thought, reluctantly opening one eye.

Dressed in blue swimming trunks, Dan grinned down at her. His body, as lean and muscular as she remembered, looked fabulous. What was that old saying? she mused. *Tall, tan, and terrific.* It fit him. He'd make her readers come back for more.

He dropped down beside her, admiring the sleek lines of her high-cut blue suit. "Hi. That's some suit."

"Why aren't I surprised to see you?" she asked, suspicious of how easily he'd found her.

"Hmmmm. That, Millie, is a less-than-enthusiastic greeting. Can't you do better for an old friend?"

Turning on her side, she dug into her bag for her wristwatch. "By my calculations, Murdock, we've known each other for about four hours, three of which were spent apart."

"Sassy woman. You know you're glad to see me."

She was, but she wasn't going to let him know that. "How's Louie?"

"Squawking mad. The judge set a high bail. Louie doesn't like his rights taken away. Neither does Spike, but he's a lot less vocal."

"Will this be on the evening news?"

"Who knows? Nabbing a two-bit crook isn't exactly earth shattering. Our work has just begun."

"Then why the high bail?"

"It isn't who you are, it's who you know. That's why."

"Will he raise it?"

He thought of Louie's threats. "I hope not. Considering Louie's record, the D.A. asked the judge to set bail at a quarter of a million. Given Louie's mob friends, he was glad to accommodate us. Even Louie doesn't have that kind of clout."

"Good. Then the Goldbergs won't worry." She relaxed. "How did you find me?"

"I'm a brilliant cop," he bragged, his boyish grin taking the conceit out of his remark.

She scuffed sand at him with her toe. "Modest, too. You should be written up. Think of the publicity."

"Not me. There's an advantage to working outside of the limelight. Can we talk about you? I see criminals all the time."

Millie hid her disappointment. She'd have to use more finesse to get Dan to agree to an interview. Smiling, she gave him the go-ahead sign.

"You have a gorgeous face."

"That's what they all say," she agreed blandly. He scowled, which pleased her. "There's something else, Murdock. You put a tail on me, didn't you?"

"Well, you wouldn't tell me where you were going." He shrugged, but his eyes were warm with admiration.

Just then a beach ball landed near his feet, spraying sand. A towheaded toddler came chugging over, tears in his eyes. When Dan gave him the ball, he patted the child on the back, praising him.

"That's a pretty terrific throw you have, young man. How about showing me how you do that?"

The pudgy youngster's face broke out in a broad smile. With his mother watching from nearby, the little boy, who solemnly confided that his name was Bobby, threw the ball. It landed a scant few feet from Dan. He showered the boy with compliments. As his mother led him away, the child called over his shoulder, "See you later."

Millie filed this new knowledge about Dan away for future reference. She told herself she was interested in him only for professional reasons. That didn't quell the warm feeling growing in the pit of her stomach. She returned to their previous conversation. "Isn't tailing innocent people a waste of taxpayer money?"

He agreed without hesitation. "It sure is, and it's all your fault. I ought to arrest you for being uncooperative." He grinned. "You could bribe me out of making the arrest, you know."

The man was mad, she thought. Kind to children, but mad nevertheless. It would be fun trailing after him for a few days to get her story. "Murdock, I think you should jump in the ocean. To quote someone I know, the exercise will do you good."

"I'm going," he said, "but you'd better know right now that I'm cooling off because of you." Without giving her a chance to recover from his bold statement, he ran down to the water and dove in.

Leaning on her elbows, she watched him swim. She noticed she wasn't the only one enjoying the sight. Other women's heads were turned in his direction. He was good, she decided. He swam effortlessly, cutting through the water with an economy of motion. After ten minutes he emerged, coming back to sink down next to her. His fingers trailed across her arm.

"Mmm, you feel good, Millie."

She rested her hand on his, stopping his exploring. "Don't." She barely recognized her own feathery voice.

"Don't what, Millie?" He lifted his head. His eyes bored into hers. "Don't tell you that I felt something back then, and that I want to see if it's real?"

"Dan, please . . ."

"We both felt something. Don't deny it."

"It doesn't matter whether we did or not. I was excited. It was dangerous. Danger and sex trigger one another. That's common knowledge."

"Not for me. You were the excitement. You were the 'danger,' not Louie."

She hesitated, surprised at the bluntness of his remark. She turned away, only to have him cup her chin, forcing her to meet his fierce gaze.

"But you're right," he said. "Sex and danger are a powerful mix. So . . ." He released her and moved back. "What shall we talk about?"

Comfortable now, she said, "Let's start with you."

He nodded. "That's easily taken care of. I'm thirty-six years old. I live alone in an old Victorian house. My parents live in Sarasota. And I've got a sister living in Hernando Beach with her husband Jack and two kids. One's a boy, aged ten; the other's a girl. She's fifteen and always in love. They live near Pine Island. Someday I'll take you there. You can walk out in the Gulf for miles without having the water reach the top of your head.

"I was an all right student in high school. Mostly, I chased girls and played poker. For a while I considered making that my life's work, until one day my dad sat me down and said, 'Deal.' He took me for every cent I had in the bank, six months' allowance, and the use of the car. After that, school was more attractive. I was a positive genius of applied fervor in college. I even won an academic scholarship during my junior and senior years. It helped pay the bills. I attended law school, but quit for personal reasons. I like my job."

"No marriage?" She wanted to know what the personal reasons were.

A shadow crossed his face. "Once, a long time ago."

She recalled his easy way with the little boy, thinking he'd make a wonderful father. "And since?"

He brushed drops of water from his forehead. "And since . . . I live the way I choose. No commitments, no promises. My line of work isn't exactly the most secure."

How could she argue with that? She'd had plenty of letters from wives and widows of policemen. "You must be hungry. Want some fruit?"

He gazed at her for a long moment. "I didn't take you for a coward, Millie," he said at last. "Don't be afraid. I'm not after anything you don't want to offer." Giving her time to absorb his meaning, he rooted around in her bag, finding a red apple. He took a big bite and munched contentedly.

"Now that I've made my life an open book," he went on, "what about you?"

She folded a towel under her head, using it as a pillow. "What about me?"

"Millie, you know what I mean. None of us materialize out of thin air. Tell me about yourself."

"I'm here on an extended visit, you might say."

He nodded. "Who are you visiting?"

"Myself. I came here from New Jersey to find me again. My husband died a little over a year ago."

He cursed quietly. "Kids?"

"No kids. End of story," she said, deliberately closing down the conversation. Dan nodded, then squeezed her hand.

A luxury cruise liner moved slowly across their line of vision. "Ever wonder where they're going?" he asked.

She was grateful he'd chosen a neutral topic. "Sure I do. Sometimes I think I'd like to be a stowaway."

Their eyes met and held. "Is there someone now you'd like to stow away with?"

"No . . . no one." Her voice was husky. She turned away from his heated gaze. Rolling onto her stomach, she dug up a handful of sand, letting the warm grains filter through her fingers.

Dan resumed eating the apple, happily making chomping noises.

"You're supposed to chew the apple quietly, Murdock."

He gave her a dazzling smile. "I know. I do it deliberately. I fool myself into thinking I'm eating a chocolate ice-cream sundae with hot fudge, whipped cream, and a cherry on top." At her look of uncertainty, he explained, "There's something about using all your senses when you eat. Makes you think you've had a wonderful meal . . . or an ice-cream sundae."

She poked his stomach, teasing. "Not the way you're doing it."

"Be quiet, sassy mouth. This is behavior modification at its best." Concentrating on the apple, he finished it, stripping the fruit to its core. Then he rooted in his shirt pocket, coming up with a fresh supply of Chiclets. He offered her the box.

"No, thanks," she said. "I've got something better." She reached into her bag and withdrew a chocolate bar dotted with nuts. She flopped over on her back, holding it high for inspection.

Dan groaned. "You're not going to eat all that by yourself, are you?"

"Why else would I be unwrapping the whole thing?" She slowly peeled off the paper.

His mouth turned downward and he pretended to pout. "You're cruel." He sucked the last of the sugar coating from the gum. "I'm on a diet."

She playfully pinched the skin at his waistline, not getting enough between her fingers to count as fat. "As well you should be," she teased. "How long have you been on this diet?"

"Going on my second week." He groaned again as she held the confection near her lips. "Don't eat that."

She took a healthy bite, then said matter-of-factly, "Statistics say you'll gain it back. It's not a matter of diet. It's a change of life-style. Habits, Murdock, habits."

He glared at her. "You're a big encouragement."

She sank her teeth into more of the chocolate. "Mmmmm. Luscious."

"Are you going to offer me any for saving your life?"

She peered up at him, then favored him with an unmerciful smile. "Daniel, it isn't polite to ask. Didn't your mother teach you that when you were a little boy?"

"My father taught me to go after whatever I wanted."

Giggling, she moved the candy bar out of his reach. "I'm sure he'd approve of my trying to keep you healthy."

She minced another tiny bite, dripping some of the rapidly melting chocolate on her finger. She licked it off like a lollipop. "Of course, if you'd like me to be party to your early demise, I could, I suppose, offer you a bite." She raised her hand to offer him some, then recanted as he came nearer. "However, in good conscience, because you saved my life, I can't take yours." She lowered the candy bar. "Sorry, Murdock, you'll just have to live vicariously, wishing you were like me. I never have to diet. Good gene pool."

Growling, he lunged at her, grabbing the chocolate bar. His mouth opened. "And here," she said with an exaggerated sigh, "I was going to offer you a meal for being so nice."

He dropped the candy onto her sand-dusted body, ruining it completely. Laughing merrily, she tossed it back into her bag and flipped onto her stomach.

"What kind of meal?" he asked.

"A home-cooked meal," she said, blithely stacking the deck in her favor. She'd feed him a good meal, serve chocolate ice cream for dessert, then casually spring her idea on him.

"What did you have in mind?" He gave her a long, smoldering look. She looked better than the sweetest, most alluring piece of chocolate. Lying as she was, her breasts plumped together above the top of her bathing suit, enticing him. That suit, he decided, was sexier than a bikini. Her skin, glistening with suntan oil, made him itch to slide up against her.

"Actually," she said, "what I had in mind was more in the way of a proposition."

"Well, now . . ." He stood up, dusting the sand from his body, then reached down to pull her up, too. One hand cupped her head. The other anchored her firmly to him. "I like a woman who knows what she wants. I'll bring the wine."

He slowly lowered his mouth to hers and kissed her lightly, almost chastely. Still, Millie felt scorched by the kiss. As she watched him stride away, she realized she would have been wiser telling him exactly what kind of proposition she had in mind.

Three

Millie phoned Wylie the moment she arrived home. For a while she couldn't tell if her agent was thrilled because Millie's creative juices were running again, or because of the story of the morning's arrest.

"Millie, he's a gift from heaven. What does he look like?"

When Millie finished describing Dan, Wylie confirmed her opinion that her readers would love to know more about the man who had shielded her from death with his life. The truth was, Millie wanted to know more about him, too.

"Reconstruct the crime," Wylie ordered. "Get policemen to play the parts of Louie and Spike if you have to."

Millie groaned. Reconstructing the scene meant putting herself beneath Dan's body again. He was already expecting a proposition.

"And be sure to take plenty of pictures."

Naturally, Wylie wanted pictures. "Wylie, how do you suggest I take pictures of us when I was hidden the whole time?"

"That shouldn't present a problem. I'll ask one of my friends down there to recommend a good cameraman. Or, if you want, you can ask the detective who was in the store to take the pictures. If Murdock is like most people, he'll jump at the chance to read about himself."

Not exactly, Millie thought. From the look on Dan's face when he'd talked about his life, she'd had the distinct impression he was a man who valued his privacy. "There are still a few details to work out."

"Oh, you mean clearing it with Port Rico's police chief. That's a mere formality. These little towns welcome all the help they can get."

Millie needed all the help she could get. One thing about her agent, she thought. Wylie barreled her way past all obstacles, seeing only what she wanted to see. In this case, a book.

"It isn't exactly that," Millie murmured, wishing she hadn't put the cart before the horse. She should have had all the arrangements made before calling Wylie.

Wylie's exasperation was evident. "Millie, what's the matter with you? Say what you mean and be done with it, for goodness' sake."

"I haven't asked him yet."

"Uh-oh."

Millie could imagine the expression on Wylie's face. She hastened to make things right.

"I'm planning to ask him tonight."

Wylie's relief was audible. So was her approval. "Tonight? You have a date with him, you tricky devil! Good for you. It's about time you took yourself out of your self-imposed celibacy. I've never been one to understand the life of a hermit."

Millie could have kicked herself. Her twin brother Kipp and his wife had been hinting the same thing recently.

"It's nothing like that," Millie said. "The truth is, I think he'll be more amenable to saying yes if I ask him on a full stomach."

Wylie's short bark of laughter ripped through the wire. "Okay, Millie. Whatever works. I have to admit I tried the same ruse once."

"And what happened?"

Wylie chorlted. "The usual. I married the guy."

Millie decided Wylie was soft where men were concerned. The only thing that had happened that morning, she told herself, was that she had been provided a fortuitous opportunity to branch out her writing. Daniel J. Murdock was the limb she'd climb on—after she pulled a little joke on him first.

The invitation was for seven o'clock. She hurried to the supermarket to buy steaks, determined to get the best money could buy. Then she stopped for fresh fruit and vegetables. Last, she went to a marvelous Italian bakery that made the best chocolate cheesecake in the world.

Watching the time, she rushed home to make a

platter of hors d'oeuvres. She marinated the steaks, then prepared a generous Caesar salad and a wild rice vegetable dish. To keep it informal, she planned to serve the meal on the small patio facing the canal. The idea was that when Dan's appetite was satiated—and he was too stuffed to protest—she'd spring her proposition on him.

She prayed Wylie was right that everyone liked a moment in the limelight. Why should Dan be any different?

Satisifed that her home was spotless, she shampooed her hair and bathed. But the scented bubble bath, which usually worked wonders at relaxing her, failed to deliver its usual magic. The thought of entertaining Dan—or any man—for whatever reason—after years of living as a married woman, set her nerves rattling.

She pulled clothes from her closet and tossed them on the bed, trying on and discarding one outfit after another. She wanted to look nice, but didn't want to look provocative. Why give Dan false ideas when he already had one whopping false idea, courtesy of her? She settled for simple white linen slacks, topped by a short-sleeved tomato red silk blouse.

By the time she had finished dressing, she regretted her rash invitation. She should have just asked him for an interview at the beach. Then she wouldn't be watching the clock every five minutes.

She nervously sprang off the couch when the doorbell rang. All right, Millie, she told herself, stop acting like a giddy adolescent about to date the big letter man on campus. This is nothing more than a polite thank-you dinner, plus a simple, straightforward business proposition. Act your age.

Dan's insistent knock sent her scurrying through the white-tiled foyer. As she swung the door open, her best-intentioned warnings flew out the window.

Trouble stood in her doorway, a lazy, lambent smile on his handsome face. Trouble handed her a bouquet of daisies, a large gold-foil-wrapped box of Perugina, and a bottle of Beaujolais.

Dan Murdock, in blue slacks and sport shirt, his thick hair neatly combed, was nothing short of a knockout. He was more handsome, if that were possible, than before. Clean shaven, he smelled of soap and musky cologne. It was evident from his appraisal of her that he expected something portentous from the evening.

"Hi. Am I too early?"

"No, no, of course not." She stepped aside, ushering him in. "You look . . . different." She inwardly cursed herself for what he must assume was a case of unwarranted and idiotic fawning.

He tilted his head to one side, amused. "Different good or different bad?"

"Different good," she admitted.

He gave an exaggerated sigh of relief. Then he studied her so intently, she blushed. "You look different, too. Not that the suit you had on today wasn't a showstopper. When I think of those legs of yours . . ."

Millie felt her heart trip at the heat blazing in

his eyes. So much for her plans not to be affected, she thought. "Come into the kitchen."

"Wait a minute." He touched her arm, making her face him. "Is this the way you say hello to a man after a hard day's work?"

"Hard day's work, my eye." She resorted to teasing as a buffer. It was easier than falling into his arms. "You spent the afternoon at the beach, the same as I did. As I recall, the hardest thing you did was try to steal my candy."

Dan skimmed his fingers over her cheek. He felt the leap of desire within him, the heavy thudding of his heartbeat. He had thought of her while they were apart. Her skin had been so soft, as soft as the petal of a delicate flower. Her perfume drew him to her.

"Not so," he said. "I never told you how my day started." He released her arm and followed her into the sunny kitchen. He stood near her as she put the box of candy on the counter.

"There was this screwball dame," he continued, "who insisted on getting herself in trouble. Scrawny thing, too." He raised his eyes to the ceiling, as if in pain. "The sacrifice I made saving her life—"

"Sacrifice?" She leaned back against the counter, not even trying to work while he was dishing out this line of malarkey. The impish glint in his eyes made her heart turn over.

"Yes, sacrifice." Her lashes were the thickest he'd ever seen. "The things I do for my job. She had a face a man wouldn't look at twice—ouch! Pinching's out."

"Twice, Murdock?"

He rubbed his arm. "Okay. Maybe I went a little overboard with the numbers. Anyhow, then I had to make sure she didn't drown in the ocean."

Millie sighed. "You poor thing. You really did have a rough day."

He nodded. "You can see how grateful I am to be away from her."

She laughed. His teasing had melted her nervous tension. "These flowers are lovely. How did you know daisies are my favorite?"

"Lucky guess. Actually, they were all the florist had. Stop changing the subject and tell me about your day. Did anything out of the ordinary happen to you?" His hand trailed up her bare arm. She pushed it away.

"Behave yourself or I'll call a cop."

"Go ahead. You'll be surprised how fast one arrives."

"Murdock, are you going to let me answer your question or what?"

He shrugged, giving her permission. "First," she began, "this crazy galoot from a TV show jerks open my car door. There I sat, idling the time away, waiting to go into Goldberg's. Anyway, this awful-looking weirdo piles into my car, waving something shiny under my nose. Then he orders me—doesn't ask, mind you—orders me out or else . . ."

Dan was watching her lips, making her forget the story she was telling. Her eyelids lowered. "Dan, this isn't fair. The flowers . . ."

He set them on the counter and slipped his

arms around her waist. "The flowers will keep. Now what were you saying?"

She wet her dry lips, and was instantly sorry when Dan's eyes darkened. "This—this big oaf knocked me down onto the seat."

"Did he have his way with you?"

He found a sensitive spot behind her ear to nuzzle. She felt it to the tip of her toes.

"Dan!"

"What? Don't you like this?" He kissed the underside of her chin. "You're gorgeous, Millie. You should always wear red." He touched a silver bangle earring. "I don't like the thought of you putting a hole in this lovely ear." His tone was unnervingly intimate.

This wasn't going to work, Millie thought. They were operating on different agendas. As soon as she posed her request he'd know she'd set him up. Why did her legs turn to jelly when she needed to walk resolutely out of the room and onto the patio?

"Hey." His voice sent a warm thrill through her. "All I'm doing is saying hello."

She thrust out her hand. "Shake. It works just as well." She wished he'd stop looking at her with those X-ray eyes. It was as if he could see her inner struggle. She resisted the urge to melt in his arms and picked up the box of candy, holding it before her like a shield. "Is this for me or you?"

He chuckled. "That depends, sassy mouth. Treat me right and I may offer you a piece. I'm not as selfish as *some* people I know."

Suddenly her stomach growled, making her blush. "Ooops."

"Don't worry about it. If I could growl on command, I'd join you. All I had to eat today was an apple. A certain piggish someone I know almost devoured a whole candy bar without sharing."

Millie closed her eyes for a moment, letting her insides adjust to the war going on. Dan's very nearness unsettled her. Dinner had been a bad idea.

"Ease up, Millie," he said. "You're too transparent." He placed his hands on her tense shoulders, sliding his fingers up the sides of her neck. "Am I the first man you've dated since your husband's death?"

She nodded. "This isn't a date. It's—it's dinner between two people who found themselves in an unusual situation."

"Millie, I'm glad I'm here. I want you to be glad, too." He rubbed his hands up and down her arms, then settled them on her shoulders. He leaned his forehead against hers. "Oh, Millie," he murmured, kissing her cheek. "What are we going to do about you?"

She drew back, managing a wry smile. "Did they teach you mind reading in detective school, Murdock?"

His response was surprisingly defensive. "What they taught me was to keep my guard up. Perhaps you can tell me why I have this unholy urge to lower it with you?"

She couldn't begin to tell him. She was having her own troubles. Starting with keeping her hands to herself. She wanted desperately to touch the scar near his lip, to ask if he'd ever been hurt in the line of duty. "Would you like to go outside?" she asked. "There's an orange and grapefruit tree in the backyard."

He laughed. "Thank you. I've seen orange and grapefruit trees before. I'm a Floridian, remember? Let me help you prepare dinner. What are we having?"

"I fixed you something special because I was such a stinker before. Cooking gives me a chance to relax, to create, to make a statement about my personality. If you eat my food, you know the real me."

She didn't let him see her broad smile as she opened the refrigerator and lifted out a plate of hors d'oeuvres. It was covered with tinfoil. Atop it lay a sprig of mint. "Could you bring that, please?" she asked, indicating a tray with two wineglasses.

"This is very nice," he said, stepping outside with her. He glanced around. "You get shade in the afternoon. Smart girl. This sun can be brutal." He set the tray down on a round table.

The covered patio was small but attractively furnished. Yellow and blue floral pillows adorned tubular chairs, a chaise, and a cozy swing. Dan chose that and patted the cushion next to him.

"I've always loved these things. Come here, Millie."

She walked over to him, uncovering the foil from the plate. "Have some. I'm very pleased with the results."

Dan's lazy smile of invitation turned to one of

questioning as he gazed at the hors d'oeuvres. It was obvious he was trying to be polite. "What are these?" The food was mostly an unappetizing white.

"Oh, they're delicious." Barely containing her mirth, she watched him tentatively pick up a cracker with white topping. He chewed it, then grabbed his wineglass.

"That's sawdust with cottage cheese," he protested, eyeing her suspiciously.

"Diet cottage cheese," she said happily. "You said you have to watch your weight. Here, try one of these." Mischievously, she chose a cracker with a sick, yellowish spread. "Low-salt cheddar cheese. or would you prefer water-packed sardines? Full of selenium."

He frowned. "I refuse to eat anything that wiggles."

She pretended to be affronted. "How can you call this dead fish alive?" Pointing to another tasteless-looking morsel, she said, "Well, if you don't want that, how about this?" She offered him a cracker topped with a green mass.

"Is a clump of grass your idea of gourmet food?"

"Watercress is very healthy for you. Full of iron."

"When I need iron, I pump it. And I'm not teething. I know how to chew, and dammit, I'm hungry. You eat it."

Millie chortled merrily. He had such a gorgeous body, she couldn't figure out why he was dieting in the first place. "Are you telling me," she asked, "that unless I feed you chewable food, you'll leave?"

He got up from the swing. "That's a dirty trick."

He glanced uncertainly at the tray. "This isn't really dinner . . . is it?"

She flopped down on the swing, laughing. He looked menacingly at her, pretending to be offended. She shook her head gleefully. Her laughter ignited his.

"Enough," she said. It felt so good to laugh, to share. She hadn't realized how much she'd missed the silliness of good plain fun. "I cooked for you. I swear on all my cookbooks."

"Not rice cakes, I hope."

Giggling, she confessed she'd really prepared steaks to broil on the barbecue. He sat beside her, and for a few minutes they enjoyed the soft sounds of the water lapping at the seawall.

"Why in the world are you dieting, Dan?" Millie asked. "You certainly don't look fat."

"Cops shouldn't be fat. Makes it harder to run."

"The newspapers will be full of this morning's events, won't they?"

He shook his head. "No, it was routine."

"But what you do isn't routine, surely. I think the public is entitled to know—"

"The public doesn't give a damn. Their attention span is about as long as it takes to change the dial on a television set. If there'd been a murder this morning, it would have made news. Nothing happened."

Except to me, she thought. "Maybe you and the public need to give a little bit."

"Meaning?"

"Meaning a good public relations campaign could

make a difference in the public's perception of your work. I realize Port Rico isn't a major city, but that's all the more reason not to be complacent."

"Frankly, that's not my concern. I do my job the way I see best. Without someone looking over my shoulder. I leave the theatrics to television." A look of annoyance crossed over his handsome features. "How we'd get from broiling steaks to this?"

She'd moved too fast. Dan wasn't ready to discuss her doing a profile on him. She put on a bright smile and stood up. "In this house the guests kibbitz in the kitchen with the help."

Dan carried the tray and the remaining hors d'oeuvres into the kitchen. Millie followed with the empty wineglasses. She washed. He rinsed.

"Do you mind if I look around your house?" he asked when they were through.

"Please."

Her home consisted of three bedrooms—one of which she apparently used as an office; a computer was set up on a table—a living room, a den, and a great room that flowed from the kitchen. The rooms surrounded her patio, which featured sliding glass doors connecting it to every interior room. The airy feeling of indoor/outdoor living was further achieved by glass-topped tables, white wicker furniture, and predominately white accents highlighting fabrics in shades of blue and mauve.

"I like it," he said, coming back after a few minutes. "Did you rent this furnished?"

"Yes. I have a three-month lease that I can renew at any time. I've been here a month."

"So you like it here?"

"I'm content."

He noted her use of the word content, not happy.

"When the realtor first showed me homes here," she went on, "I thought a split meant a split-level house. I didn't know it meant having the master bedroom wing separated from the rest of the house."

"Yes. People in Florida tend to have a lot of company. This floor plan gives everyone privacy. Of course, if a couple has a baby, the baby's room can be far away." Dan hesitated, then decided to push. He was intrigued by this woman. "Why didn't you ever have children, Millie?"

The memories of the endless trips to doctors washed over her. She and Frank had tried everything, but his sperm count had been too low. She'd loved him too much to let him know how anguished she'd been at not having a child.

"The time never seemed right," she said, tossing her hair back, over her shoulder. The defensive look in her eye gave him his answer.

She took the pan of marinated steaks out of the refrigerator and handed it to him. "How are you at grilling steaks?"

"Didn't I tell you it's one of my specialties?"

He donned the chef's apron she gave him, then lit the grill while she finished setting the table.

"Don't look now," he said, "but I think we have a visitor." A heron, moving its long neck in slow-motion time to its equally long, skinny legs, was walking toward them. It stopped and cocked its head. His long, tapered bill opened so slowly that Dan laughed. "Fast critter."

"Come here, Henry," Millie called. She held out an anchovy from the Caesar salad. The heron made its way toward her so slowly, she finally walked over to him.

"Henry?" Dan asked dubiously.

"Yes. We've kind of adopted each other. Henry is a beggar. If anyone along the canal is fishing, Henry waits. No one can resist his begging."

"He's certainly fat."

"He likes chocolate." She smirked, darting out of Dan's reach when he tried to swat her rump with a towel.

"Hey," he said, "I think Henry's in love."

Millie followed his gaze. "Oh, she's beautiful." A white heron, her feathers swept back along her trim body, had made her way to Henry's side. Seeing the two of them standing side by side filled Millie's eyes with tears. "They look so right together, don't they? I'm going to call her Henrietta." She smiled. "Henry and Henrietta Huggins. What do you think?"

"I think you're an adorable nut. Dinner's ready."

The steaks were cooked to perfection. It was a perfect night, Dan thought, watching Millie as she talked animatedly about the area. Boats rocked gently at their moorings near the docks. The sky darkened, leaving dusk for another day. Stars filled the sky, glittering brightly.

"At home," Millie said, her soft voice filled with awe, "it's so populated and we have so many lights, we don't see the stars this clearly. Certainly not this many." She lifted her face toward the sky. "Beautiful, isn't it?"

He gazed at her exquisite profile. She was enough to distract any man. "You're beautiful," he murmured. He wanted nothing more than to hold her in his arms again, but he sensed she wasn't ready. He heard her small, pleased intake of breath at his compliment. It was enough for now. "I never wanted to live in a big city," he went on. "There's too much of everything. Too much pollution, too many people."

The doorbell rang, surprising them both. Millie opened the door and Ben Jackman, his face grim, came in.

"Ben," Dan said. "What are you doing here?"

Ben glanced at Millie, then turned back to Dan. "Louie's made bail."

Dan emitted a string of curses. Millie looked from one man to the other. Both were tall, both commanded attention, but where Dan's longer dark hair and graying temples gave him a slightly weathered look, Ben's close-cropped hair and freckles made him seem youthful. There were deep laugh lines near his green eyes. As Dan made the introductions he extended his hand in greeting and smiled. A bright, open smile.

Millie liked him immediately, but her attention was riveted on Dan. He had changed before her eyes. Gone was the teasing manner, the easy, comfortable air. He was once again the intensely committed detective, concerned first and foremost for the public's welfare.

"We'd better get over to the Goldbergs'," Dan said.

As they turned to go, Millie touched his arm. "Wait a minute."

"What for?" he asked, now all business, letting her know he was focused on leaving.

"I'll go with you."

"Sorry, Millie," he said with implacable finality. "You'd get in the way. I always work alone. I thought you understood that from our conversation."

She understood all too clearly. She'd failed.

Four

Outside Millie's house, Dan jammed his fists into his pockets. So much for weeks of hard work, he thought, kicking up a spray of pebbles. Thinking about the turnstile way the mob made a mockery of justice infuriated him.

Dan and Ben quickly got into the car and clicked on their seat belts. Over the years, they had developed a camaraderie, easing the tensions of their daily routine. Tonight, however, there was none of the usual trading of banter and stories. The atmosphere was subdued. Dan slouched down in his seat, one knee jammed up against the door. He stared out the window.

Ben broke the silence at last. "You were a little short with the lady back there, you know."

Dan, startled by the unwonted reprimand, swiveled his head toward Ben. "What are you talking about?"

Ben glanced at him. "Seems to me all Millie wanted to do was help. And what's this garbage about working alone? What am I? Your chauffeur?"

"Oh, come on, Ben. I didn't mean you or other police personnel. Millie's a civilian. She's got no business being with us. Suppose Louie had gotten a good look at her face? Then where would she be? I'll tell you. Stuck in her house under police protection, same as the Goldbergs are going to be."

When they stopped for a red light, Ben lit a cigarette. Trails of smoke curled upward. "Is that why you're attracted to her? Because she won't take orders?"

Dan gnawed his bottom lip. He was dying for a cigarette. "Who said I'm attracted to her?"

"Hey, are we playing blindman's buff, pal? You were there, weren't you? And you did have her tailed today."

His life was an open book. "That was strictly business. Anyway, Mike was off duty. He owed me a favor," Dan argued lamely. He'd never been able to con Ben. "She's just a woman I met today who happens to be interesting. That's all."

At Ben's snort, Dan chafed. "Knock it off. She's really a very intelligent woman."

"That's what I said. She's just a nice, intelligent woman you met today. And her little dinner party was designed for you both to exchange compliments about your respective brain power." Ben stubbed out his cigarette. "What does this intelligent woman do for a living?"

"How do I know? It didn't come up." All he knew was that she was a widow. What *did* she do? he wondered, remembering the computer.

"All right," Ben said. "Stop jumping down my throat. What do we do now?"

"Offer comfort and protection to the Goldbergs, and hope Louie makes a mistake, so we can pull him in again. Ask me, Spike's about ready to cooperate, don't you think?"

Ben turned onto the Goldbergs' street. "He might need another day, but I agree. He's mad Louie's out. Dan, you should finish law school. Maybe you could figure out a way for some of these collars and convictions to stick."

Shoulda, woulda, coulda. Dan reran his reason for not finishing school. Because it had been more important to give Lana a start. And he honestly enjoyed his work with the force. He found it exhilarating, although lately he had been thinking more and more about returning to law school. Getting the sheepskin.

"Don't talk about the past, Ben." Dan gritted his teeth and wished for a perfect world. "We're short staffed at the department as is. John Q. Public isn't exactly banging down our doors to give us a budget that will let us hire a public relations consultant."

"What for?"

"You know the chief. He's got some crazy notion that if big cities use public relations firms to boost their cause, then we should, too. Ask me, the chief's wrong. I say let well enough alone."

Both men shook their heads. "And I thought all we had to worry about were the criminals."

Dan laughingly agreed. "Did you ask Natalie if she'll work the double shift?"

Natalie Gershon was a twenty-four-year-old police officer who'd followed the tradition started by her father and two older brothers. They were in police work in neighboring communities.

"Yeah, the little pumpkin said no problem. She wants to build up vacation days."

"Isn't it about time you quit calling her that? Have you looked at her lately? She's all grown-up."

Ben stopped in front of the Goldbergs' and turned off the ignition. "I've been calling her little pumpkin since she was knee-high to a grasshopper and her brothers and I were on the same high school football team. Natalie will always be little pumpkin to me."

"What you don't know about women could fill a book," Dan said as they strode up the stone pathway.

"Look who's talking. I'm not the one who forgot to thank his hostess for a good meal tonight, old buddy."

Dan slapped his forehead with his palm. "I'll call her tomorrow and set it right." He had been planning to call her anyway, but Ben didn't have to know everything.

As she cleared away the remnants of their meal, Millie thought about Dan's curt refusal when she'd impulsively asked to accompany him. He had bluntly told her he worked alone. Well, she'd just have to change his mind. Since when did a temporary roadblock stop her? she mused, feeling more like the old Millie, who used to play outrageous pranks on and with her twin brother Kipp. But what would work best on Dan?

She mulled over her options as she scooped out small pieces of tuna from a can she kept ready for Henry. She dropped bits of leftovers onto the edge of the patio. The birds cautiously ventured near.

Birds . . . water . . .

That's it! she decided with a sudden victorious whoop. "Thank you, darlings. You're my inspiration."

She hurried into her office and worked on her column, readying three weeks' worth of advice to send to the paper. Then she washed, undressed, and slipped into bed. Her mind at ease, she fell instantly asleep.

The phone jarred her awake at 7:00 A.M. Groping for it, she figured it was either Kipp, checking in, or Wylie. She fervently hoped it was Kipp.

"How'd it go?" The voice was feminine, definitely Brooklyn.

Millie groaned. Starting the day with Wylie was like being poked awake by a drill sergeant. "Wylie, are we in the same time zone? I know you can't be in your office yet. Do you realize I've spoken to you more in the last two days than I normally do in months?" She propped the pillow behind her head.

"I couldn't wait. What did Dan say? I'm dying to

know how the evening went. Who's going to do the photography?"

Millie coughed nervously. "It's probably a good idea not to count on Dan."

"In other words, he refused."

"Not exactly. I never had the opportunity to ask him. We were interrupted by Ben Jackman, his partner."

Wylie sighed. "I hope your plan is foolproof, Millie. I hate to put you under stress, but after we spoke yesterday I had a call from the publisher. They're threatening to scrap the book if we don't send them something. They have a schedule, too. I went through the usual delaying tactics, but they didn't buy it this time. They politely but firmly told me a year to mourn Frank was enough. Then they followed up with if you're able to write your Ask Ms. M column, you should be able to meet your commitment with them. Honey, I have to agree. It's time."

Millie felt terrible. Wylie rode shotgun for her when she needed her, and she'd let her agent down. With new resolve she promised, "I'll get Dan to come around. I've thought of a great plan." She explained it to Wylie, who, practical to the end, asked the logical question.

"Why beat around the bush? The shortest distance between two points is a straight line. Or," she asked, inspired, "do you need an excuse to see this guy socially?"

"Never," Millie protested, a trifle too forcefully. "Neither one of us is interested in a commitment."

"Got that far, did you?"

Millie kicked off the covers and sat up. It was going to be one of those days. She swung her legs off the bed and paced the room with the phone.

"You have a one-track mind, Wylie. For your information, aside from a few laughs, Dan and I are as different as night and day."

Wylie's laughter came through loud and clear. "That's what I said. Opposites attract."

Millie took the bull by the horns and phoned Dan. He wasn't in his office. A woman named Natalie Gershon answered the phone.

"I'm glad to speak with you, Millie. You made quite an impression on our Dan. He told us how helpful you were yesterday morning."

Dan had given her credit for helping! she thought. That was a good sign. It meant he might change his mind and allow her to ride with him while she gathered research. It would only be for a week at the most. Then, blushing furiously, she wondered if while he dished out his praise, he had also explained what she had done specifically to help!

She left a message for him to call. He did so that afternoon and apologized for not thanking her for the wonderful dinner. When she broached the idea of completing their interrupted date, he immediately agreed.

"Don't bring a thing," she said, "and be here by eight. We'll get an early start."

"Where to?" he asked. His deep, masculine voice still sent shivers up her spine.

"That's the surprise," she answered, dangling the bait.

"Animal, vegetable, or mineral?"

She laughed, happy to get a nibble. "All three."
Before he could ask more questions, she hung up
and put her telephone answering machine on. No
sense pulling in the line too soon.

Millie rushed to the door when Dan rang the
bell early Sunday morning. He was dressed in
light khaki slacks and a white T-shirt. His deep tan
contrasted magnificently with his silvered temples, making him a dashing figure. He'd be a
photographer's dream, she thought. A woman's,
too. . . .

She wore a short lavender jumpsuit that zipped
up the front. He tugged on the silver loop at the
top of the zipper, effectively halting her from turning around. His eyes showed his appreciation of
her as he slowly surveyed her from head to toe.

"Where are we going?" he asked, finishing his
appreciative appraisal.

"I have a surprise for you." She smiled imp-
ishly. "You haven't eaten yet, have you?"

"No. Where's my surprise?" He expected her to
pull him into the kitchen for another home-cooked
meal.

She tugged him out onto the patio instead. A
warm breeze blew gently against their faces.

"There," she said, ready to share her excitement. She spread both arms out in front of her,
pointing proudly in the direction of the canal.
"Isn't she beautiful?"

She was a boat. A canary-yellow boat with an
outboard motor and a freeboard deep enough to
stow fishing gear. A twenty-footer.

"Whose is it?" He hoped they were going to be alone.

"Ours!" she boasted grandly.

"Ours?"

"For the whole day." She gave him a provocative, untrustworthy grin. "During dinner the other night you said you love to fish, so I planned this especially for you. It's all arranged, down to the sandwiches and drinks."

The boat was compact, Dan mused. It would keep them in constant proximity. He had visions of a perfect day.

Millie reminded him of a little girl trying to contain herself as she impulsively threw her arms around his neck.

"I knew you'd like it," she said.

He folded his arms behind her back. "I love it. Thanks."

"Come on, then," she said, easing away from him. Once again she wondered if her invitation had been a bad idea. Her body seemed ready to burst into flames whenever she was near him. She had to forcibly remind herself she was on a mission.

"You've done this often?" he asked.

"You bet. I love it. We'll be out of here and fishing in no time."

He smiled. To each his own, he thought. What he planned to fish for was a mermaid named Millie.

She skipped down the steps to the boat, calling over her shoulder, "Dan, the food chest, please? It's on the patio table."

The herons seemed to sense a picnic. "Is this a family outing, Millie? Do we take the children?"

Good idea, she thought. They'd add a festive and comic touch. She could use all the help she could get.

"Sure, why not?"

They made a strange quartet, Millie skipping to the boat, Dan lugging the food chest, and the herons gracefully bringing up the rear in slow motion.

"It'll be good for you to get away from phones and work," she said as they clambered aboard. "There's nothing like the curative powers of a day at sea." And, she hoped, it would make him more amenable to what she had in mind.

"What are you doing?" he asked, with more than a little interest as she lowered the zipper on her jumpsuit.

"What does it look like? I'm going to work on my tan."

Beneath the jumpsuit she had on the sleek, high-cut blue bathing suit she'd worn at the beach. He didn't know which he enjoyed more: her long, long legs, or the hint of breast peeking out from the top of the suit.

Her hair shimmered in the sun. She reminded him of a long-legged, suntanned sprite. She was laughing at Henry and Henrietta as they settled themselves on the bow of the boat, waiting for the fun to begin.

"I've thought of everything, Dan. We've got fishing rods. The bait tank's over the side. I'll pick it up as soon as you lift anchor. Isn't this fun?"

He could think of only one more way to have a lot of fun, and it didn't include an audience of hungry herons.

"I'll drive," she announced.

"Be my guest." Sitting down, Dan stretched his legs out and leaned back on the railing. To his pleasant surprise, she handled the boat like an old salt, explaining she'd spent summers on Long Beach Island in New Jersey.

The ocean was calm, and the boat rocked gently. Dan enjoyed relaxing and watching her, until the urge to be near her was too strong.

"Need help?" he asked, coming closer to her.

"Sit back and enjoy the scenery."

"I am."

He slipped his arms around her waist. Startled, she turned. His eyes were intense as he stared at her mouth. Then he lowered his head and kissed her softly. Sighing, she pulled back.

"Dan, I planned this day for you to relax."

"I am relaxing," he said. "At least for now. If I stay this close to you, I'm not sure how relaxed I'll be in a minute or so. Shall we try an experiment?"

His thumbs traced the line of her jaw, moving upward to her lips. "What experiment?" she asked, trying not to respond to that light caress.

"I stay here and we see which one of us stays relaxed the longest."

For a brief moment she almost played along. Then she drew back. "Dan, be fair. Remember, you're an officer of the law."

He grinned. "Which is why I'm off duty today.

I'm a civilian, with all the desires of a man off duty."

"It's not even noon yet," she protested. If he kept this up she'd forget her reason for inviting him. "Here." She moved aside. "Your turn."

She sat down on the bench, her face lifted to the sun. This was relaxing, she thought. And the farther they got from land, the less urgent her desire to interview Dan became. She recalled Wylie's suggestion that Millie had concocted this fishing trip just so she could see Dan again. Nonsense, she thought. But she didn't believe herself.

"Where do you want to drop anchor?"

She sat up, shading her eyes with her hand. "Kind of over there." She pointed to a group fishing boat. "Might as well use their radar."

"Girl after my own heart," he said approvingly.

She scampered over to the fishing rods while Dan dropped anchor. "Okay, Dan, time to fish. I'll even let you bait the hook. Show me how you do it." Make the man show his skill, she thought. Wylie would approve.

Several minutes later she had the first bite. Dan genially shouted that it wasn't fair for the guest not to get the first bite. He yelled encouragment to her as the rod bowed dangerously under the weight of the fish. "Don't drop him. Give the line more slack. No, dammit, Millie, that's not the way to do it! More slack!"

She wanted to shout back at him that she'd won many a fishing trophy. Wylie's image floated in front of her face. She heard her saying, "Dope

. . . give him the damned pole. Have you lost sight of your goal? You're after a story, not a fish."

"Dan," she said, breathing hard, "take the rod. Please. I haven't the strength to reel him in."

"Sure you do, honey." He stood behind her, bracing her. Covering her hands with his, he gave her the added power she needed. "You can do it, Millie," he said. "That fish has your name on it."

As he spoke, a large sea bass broke the water.

Millie screamed, then bit her lip in concentration. Dan was having a hard time paying attention to the bass. Millie's derrière was pressed against him. Each time she wiggled he wanted to take the fishing rod and throw it down into the boat.

They worked as a team, letting slack out of the line, then bending to reel the fish in, repeating the process over and over until the bass was close to the boat.

"Hold him, Millie. I'll get the gaff."

"He's gorgeous!" she exclaimed as he lifted the fish from the water. She threw her arms around Dan's neck, kissing him soundly. "Thank you."

He put the gaff down and caught her to him. His hands swept up her arms and down her spine. His tongue plunged into her mouth on a foray of discovery. The people from the party boat, who had been watching, clapped and shouted their approval.

Millie knew she was hearing voices. At that moment she didn't care if they were coming from inside her head or from outer space. She forgot about her mission. She knew only that Dan's encouragement, his helpfulness in making sure she had the pleasure of the first catch, and now his kiss of approval all worked on her. She felt free and wonderful for the first time in a year.

He released her slowly. For a moment they stared at each other, both aware something had changed between them, yet neither sure of what to do about it. At last, Millie moved away.

"I'm starved," she said, laughing nervously.

They spent the afternoon loafing, talking about nothing in particular, and eating. When they got hot, they jumped overboard and swam. Back on deck, Dan insisted she slather herself with sunblock. She obediently lay down on her stomach so he could apply lotion to her back and shoulders. That was a mistake. Her nerves were warring once more with her common sense. It was time to try her proposition again.

"Dan, has anyone ever interviewed you about your work?"

"A few reporters have called the office from time to time." He continued to gently massage her back.

"I'd love to read what they wrote about you."

"You can't." He leaned over her, his hands trailing up and down her spine.

"Why not?" she asked, telling herself to cool it. *Disregard his hands and pay attention to business.*

"There are no articles. I turned them all down."

She shifted onto her side. "Whatever for?"

"Because I'm not interested in reading about me and I sure as hell don't think anyone else will be, either."

"I disagree." She eased into her speech carefully. "Imagine if people knew about the arrest the other day. You were a hero. It's a great story."

"You're right. But what happened between you and me is private. Or don't you care?"

It was great theater, she thought, but she saw his point. She also saw her book going down the drain, and the advance money, which she had already spent, having to be returned. She remembered Wylie's sage suggestion about the shortest distance between two points.

"But, Dan, if it were reported correctly—"

"Millie, what do you do for a living?" he asked suddenly.

"I'm a writer," she admitted.

He frowned. "Newspaper?"

"Yes."

"And you saw a story in me?"

"Something like that," she said, feeling her way through a partial explanation. "Surely a little friendly publicity can't hurt."

Dan's face reflected his opinion. "Talk to my chief. His name is Peter Wasach. He'd probably jump at the chance, but leave me out of it."

"But he's not the one I'm interested in," she protested, wondering what made Dan so averse to publicity.

Dan carefully capped the bottle of lotion and wiped his hands. "Then the real reason for all this"—he waved his hand to encompass the boat, the fishing rods, the food in the ice chest—"is your interest in writing about me?"

Millie sat up. It was going all wrong, falling apart in bits and pieces. "Don't put it that way, Dan. I didn't need to spend all this money and hire a boat just to ask you a question." Which was precisely what she had done, she admitted silently. From the look of disapproval on Dan's face, she guessed he could see right through her. "What's wrong with combining business with pleasure?"

He scowled. "Nothing, as long as both people know what's going on. I was under the impression this was strictly pleasure."

She wanted to say it was, but bit her tongue. She did want to interview him, yet she couldn't deny she wanted more. And that still unnerved her.

From then on, a pall hung over them. They made small talk. Millie knew she'd hit a brick wall. Dan knew he'd been taken. And quite possibly, he thought, the other night's meal fell into the same category as today's outing. While he was thinking about her in amorous terms, she'd only been interested in him as a means to an end.

"It's time we headed in, Millie," he said at last. "I'm working the four-to-twelve shift tonight."

He was lying, she thought. He'd told her he had the day off. Wylie would be thrilled to hear how her client had bombed out, Millie thought ruefully.

She nodded her agreement, and Dan turned the boat toward home. The herons lifted from the water and flew back to land, leading the way.

The birds had been the only winners, Millie thought glumly. At least they could eat fish. She had to eat crow. For the second time, she had blown her opportunity with Dan.

She wasn't giving up, though. If there was one thing Millie Gordon never walked away from, it was a challenge. Somehow, she'd figure out a way to make him change his mind.

Five

Dan leaned over the desk, his face tight with emotion. He was stunned by Police Chief Wasach's suggestion.

"Get someone else. I've already said no."

Wasach shot Dan his rarely used but highly effective I'm-the-boss look. At fifty-five, he'd been the head of the department for ten years. Dan liked him. Mostly because, he realized, until now he'd left Dan alone to do his work.

"Can't get anyone else." Wasach's tone was determined. "She wants you, tiger, and it's good public relations. Which, I might add, fell into our laps. Don't you want to help the department out?"

Dan felt as if he were acting in a bad movie. How could Millie do this to him? The shock of her request was wearing off, but not the disappointment. He'd come so close to really caring for her. He should have realized on the boat yesterday when she was peppering him with department-related questions that she had an ulterior motive and probably wouldn't give up until she got what she wanted. And she wanted plenty.

"Don't lay that guilt-trip on me, Pete. Nothing in my job description says I have to do this."

"It's no guilt-trip—and I realize it goes against your wishes—but I want you to reconsider." He turned on his persuasive voice. "I'm hoping the favorable publicity will make the city council sit up and take notice at budget time. We need some new patrol cars, not the recycled ones we've been driving. You said yourself the air conditioning is on the fritz in your car. Multiply that with dozens of other logistical and vehicular problems and you get my meaning."

"But why me? Ask one of the others. Ask Natalie. Two women should get on better."

Wasach shook his head. "Nope. You're our great white hope, Dan. Thanks to you, people nationwide will better appreciate what we do, and for free. You can't buy that kind of exposure."

"Nationwide?" The hairs on the back of Dan's neck bristled.

"Yeah. I tell you the woman's got clout."

"What in blazes are you talking about?" Dan asked, momentarily baffled. Did more bad news await him?

Wasach tossed a copy of the St. Petersburg *Clarion* across the desk. "She's syndicated. Page one, second section."

Dan dropped the first section on top of the

desk. He skimmed the page Wasach had referred to, but found nothing with Millie's byline.

Wasach leaned over the desk and tapped the paper with his finger. "Millie Gordon's really Ask Ms. M. How about that?"

Millie, a syndicated columnist. How about that, indeed. He'd shot off his big mouth to her. He'd told her about his marriage, his dropping out of law school.

He groaned, feeling a fresh surge of disappointment at the confirmation that all she wanted from him was a press-worthy tidbit.

How had she gotten to Wasach so quickly? She had spent yesterday with him. Wasach hadn't been on duty. If she'd come in to see the chief today, Ben or one of the others would have told him. "How'd you find out who she is?"

"A woman named Wylie McGuiness called me from New York." Wasach stroked his chin. "That was some piece of work, Murdock, landing on top of a famous person." A chuckle escaped him.

"Who's Wylie McGuiness?" Dan asked. Everything that had happened between Millie and him in the car was apparently now coast-to-coast common knowledge. The whole episode, locker room fodder.

"McGuiness is Gordon's agent. Do the interview, Murdock," Wasach pleaded. "Get us on the map. McGuiness is shrewd. The way she explained it, it's a case of you scratch my back, I'll scratch yours. 'Course, you also get your name in the book. That's part of the deal. You're going to be promoted as a hometown celebrity. You may even get a guest shot or two on TV."

Dan skipped past the celebrity nonsense. "Book? What are you talking about?"

"The one Gordon is writing," Wasach explained, obviously hoping patience would win Dan's cooperation. "I don't know why you're so annoyed, Murdock. Gordon's book's entitled *Not-Your-Run-of-the-Mill People.* It's about fascinating people doing fascinating jobs. For some reason this dame thinks you're a candidate for fascinating. Beats me what she sees in you."

Dan cursed, quietly but thoroughly. "Does Millie know her agent called?" He'd give her the benefit of the doubt.

Wasach steepled his fingers beneath his chin. "How do I know? I'm no mind reader. She'd have to, though, wouldn't she? All I know is that I've given permission for this Millie Gordon to ride with you for a week. Show her the ropes. Let her see what the job entails. She'll do an honest job of reporting."

Dan closed his eyes for a second. "It's a bad move. If by any chance she gets hurt, what then? Do we wait to be sued by her paper, her publisher, her agent, not to mention Millie herself?" He shook his head in disgust, not caring what the chief thought.

His superior, however, was only thinking about his goal. "Stop being so melodramatic, hotshot. Nothing's going to happen. You'll be there to protect her. From what I hear, anyway, you're pretty good at that."

"Louie's still walking the streets. Suppose he sees her with me? He's been threatening revenge."

Wasach wasn't worried. "He won't. He's not about to violate bail, not if he wants to stay out until his trial. He's got a smart attorney."

Dan frowned. "I disagree. If he hears Spike Harvey's started singing, he'll do something stupid, attorney or no attorney. Louie's more afraid of the mob than of us."

Wasach considered Dan's argument, then offered a compromise.

"I doubt he'll be a problem, but if it eases your mind we'll watch Louie for a while. As for Millie Gordon, do the easy stuff."

"Like what? Deliver babies?" Dan asked sarcastically.

"You did it once, you can do it again. By the way, how is your namesake?"

The glacial expression on Dan's face softened momentarily. "The kid's fine," he said, a note of pride in his voice. "He's seven and doing pretty well in school, last time I checked."

Dan had delivered infant Daniel Lopez seven years ago when he answered an emergency call from the Lopez home. The grateful parents, Manuel and Rosita, had named the strapping eight-pound six-ounce boy after him. Over the years he had kept in touch with the family. Rosita was pregnant again, hoping for a girl this time. The baby was due in two weeks.

"Dan," Wasach said kindly, "I know you believe I'm on the wrong track, with this publicity thing. But think what a morale booster it would be for the staff." He paused, then added carefully, "It wasn't publicity that got your Uncle Jack fingered by the mob when he was working vice in New York."

Dan didn't want to talk about it. His uncle had been gunned down in cold blood. As if that weren't bad enough, Internal Affairs had later proved his father's brother was one of what they called the bad cops. "Murdock On The Take!" It had made all the locals. Since then, keeping his family name clean and out of the news was important to Dan not only for his sake, but out of consideration for his parents.

All that slipped from his mind, though. Now he wanted to see Millie and straighten out this nonsense once and for all. He left the chief's office in a foul mood. Knowing it was better to see Millie with a calm, cool head, he decided he'd go to the cafeteria for coffee. Ben spotted him and carried a sandwich and coffee to his table.

"What's up?" Ben asked. "You look like you're ready to spit."

Dan told him about Millie and her agent and Wasach. "So, what do you think I should do?"

"Go for it, fella."

Ben's response didn't put Dan in a better frame of mind. He glared balefully at his partner and best buddy. "So much for friendship and loyalty."

"You're welcome." Ben picked up the *Clarion*, then let out a low whistle. "You lucky stiff. I wish someone would write about me."

Natalie entered the cafeteria, her green eyes sparkling. She was a tiny woman, barely tall enough to pass the standard for police officer. Her blond curls bobbed as she sat down with them. She squeezed Dan's hand. "What do you know? We have a real celeb in our midst."

"Bad news travels fast," Dan muttered.

"Hi, little pumpkin." Ben leaned over and slipped his arm around her shoulders.

"Oh, shut up, Ben."

"What's gotten into her?" Ben asked, shaking his head as Natalie stood up and stalked off.

"You figure it out," Dan said. "I've got my own troubles."

Ben was thoughtful for a moment, then said, "I may not know much, but I sure as heck know when a woman's got a man by the tail. You've got a case for this Millie. Why fight it?"

"Don't you get tired of giving advice?"

Ben grinned. "Nope. I think you're nuts. If I had the opportunity to spend a week with a woman I liked, I sure wouldn't be complaining. I'd figure out a way to make it work for me."

Dan leaned back in his chair considering Ben's advice. It wasn't hard to recall the image of Millie reeling in that bass, her body tucked firmly into his, her hair flying in the wind as she squealed with delight. Nor was it difficult to remember her flinging her arms around him and kissing him with abandon after she landed the fish.

"You would, huh?" he asked Ben.

"Damn right," Ben said, munching his sandwich.

Dan drained his coffee in two gulps. "You're not as dumb as you look. Thanks, pal."

"You're welcome, I think. What are you going to do?"

Dan crumpled his napkin and stood up. "Why, I'm going to be a hero."

Ben looked puzzled. "Am I missing the connection? I thought this was about getting Millie and you together."

Dan grinned. "It is—on my terms."

Listening to Wylie's explanation, Millie cringed. "Oh, Wylie," she wailed. "You didn't."

"I had to. What's the big deal? His boss is thrilled to death. I knocked his socks off."

"The big deal," Millie said heatedly, "is that you've done something in my interest that isn't in Dan's. He made his wishes clear on the boat." Millie recalled how their excursion had ended. "What was Dan's reaction?" she asked, dreading the answer.

"He wasn't in the office, so he doesn't know yet. I had to do it, Millie. I pitched him to the publisher. It was the only way to save the book deal, believe me. They're thrilled and can't wait to see some material."

Millie shuddered. If it weren't for the advance money already spent, she'd chuck the whole project. "Two days ago they were threatening to cancel the contract and today they're thrilled? How come?"

"Publishers are crazy. You know that. They'll say anything to get what they want."

And sometimes, Millie thought darkly, well-meaning agents, too.

• • •

Millie's doorbell rang an hour later. She guessed it was Dan. Almost reluctantly, she opened the door. Dan brushed by her, a copy of the *Clarion* in his fist. His gaze raked over her. "Did you have to pull rank?"

She sighed. She already had a headache from the phone call with Wylie. "I didn't pull anything, Dan." He was silent as he stalked into the living room. She followed him. "I'm sorry about all this. I had no idea Wylie would call your boss."

"Yeah." He shoved the paper at her. "You could have fooled me, Millie, or should I call you Ms. M?"

She was tired of being sentenced without a trial and stiffened her spine. "Millie will do fine."

He stared at her for a moment, then his gaze dropped to her mouth, forcing her to remember. "You told your agent what happened in the car?"

She blushed. With little effort she could feel his lips on hers. "Only as it pertained to the case."

"Yesterday, why didn't you come right out and ask me instead of pussyfooting around?"

"I tried to, but if you will recall, you closed out the conversation."

"That's why you wanted to go with me to the Goldbergs when Ben came by the other night, isn't it? You wanted to get information for your story." His intent gaze dared her to be up-front.

Millie could feel the tension rising between them. She rubbed her hands together. "No," she said hesitantly. "Well . . . in a way. I like the Goldbergs. I thought if they saw a familiar face it might help them. And, yes," she added, flaring suddenly, "it would have helped me with background information, too."

"Thank you for being honest, Millie. I was merely curious." His voice was as cool as if he were talking to a stranger, not someone he'd kissed fewer than twenty-four hours ago.

"I imagine you've learned what you came for," she said. She started toward the hallway. His hand on her arm stopped her. She flinched.

"Relax, Millie, I'm not going to jump you."

How could she relax when he stared at her like that? she wondered. She was tense, and she knew it showed. She'd like nothing better than to feel his hands on her neck and shoulders, massaging away the tight kinks. She lowered her lashes, not wanting him to see the flash of desire in her eyes.

"Millie?" he said huskily. She looked up. Their eyes met and clung, giving her the odd sensation of being suspended in time. He cleared his throat. "Pete wants you to ride with me for the week."

"You could refuse. I wouldn't blame you."

His tone hardened. "I want to, believe me. But the chief thinks the publicity will make the city council sit up and take notice. The department's budget has been squeezed lately."

"I see." She saw all too clearly. He was saddled with her. "Then what do you propose?"

"A truce."

Her heart skipped a beat. A truce would give her time. Time to be with him and get the book started. She was weak-kneed with relief.

"Just so we understand each other: I accept

that this is strictly business on your part, that whatever transpired between us happened because of circumstances," Dan said softly.

What could she say? she wondered. She'd gotten what she wanted, and in the process had lost more than she'd gained. She wanted to turn the clock back. She wished he'd put his arms around her and kiss her the way he had on the boat. With a sinking feeling, she waited for him to continue.

Dan shoved his hands into his pockets. He'd given her an opening to contradict him, had hoped she would. When she didn't, he went through the motions.

"I'll lay out the ground rules. If trouble starts and I say get down, I mean exactly that. I can't have you bleeding on my hands."

"Agreed," she said formally.

"If we have to go out of town to follow a lead on a case, I don't want to hear any complaints."

"Agreed."

He cleared his throat. "There may be times when you'll have to act as my partner. . . ."

Her face became animated. "You mean that? I'll actually be doing real police work with you?"

He shook his head. "No, of course not. You'll only pretend. On certain jobs, Natalie usually comes with me, but I can't have two women in the car. It'll look strange, since it isn't by the book."

"What sort of pretending?"

"We may need to pretend to be man and wife—if we have to spend a night at a motel."

She gulped. She hadn't considered spending

the night with Dan. "Is this kind of thing usually done?"

His mouth curved in a brief smile. "Only when necessary."

She hastened to agree to his conditions before he put an end to the entire deal. "All right."

"Good." He turned to leave. "And"—he casually slipped in the caveat—"I get to approve what you write about me."

Her chin shot up at that. It was enough she'd agreed to his terms like an obedient puppy, but now he was intruding on her professional integrity. Her temper sizzled. She'd always been honest and fair. She'd let him read it, of course, but for verification, not editorial consent. She made no effort to hide her mounting anger. "See here—"

"Take it or leave it," he challenged, holding his breath.

Millie mentally reviewed her options, admitting to herself her position was weak. Dan Murdock held all the cards. It *was* a question of take it or leave it. She inclined her head, then bit out the alien acceptance. "Agreed."

Did she imagine it or did she see a slight twitching of his lips? Forget it, she thought. Dan was stone-faced.

"Fine," he said. "I'll call you when I need you. Be ready to roll at a moment's notice. Police tend to keep odd hours."

"But don't you work shifts? Surely you know your own hours. Suppose I'm in the middle of a column?"

He smiled. "That's your problem, isn't it? You're the one who got your agent to arrange this."

"I told you that I didn't know Wylie was going to call your chief." She jammed her fists onto her hips. Angry as she was now, she couldn't help but remember the feel of Dan's body pressed close to hers as she reeled in the fish, the feel of his hands as they applied the sunblock to her bare skin.

He was gone before she could protest or negotiate terms. She could hardly blame him—he'd been neatly finessed by his chief.

But so had she been. Then again, all they had to do was spend one week together. What could happen in one week?

The next day at two A.M. he knocked on her door. At first Millie thought she'd left the television on. When the knock persisted, she stumbled from bed and peered out the window. The street lamp shone on a familiar car. Oh my gosh! she thought. Dan hadn't been kidding when he'd said be ready at a moment's notice.

Still groggy, she stumbled out of her bedroom. She flung open the door, oblivious to the fact that she was wearing a diaphanous white gown. "What are you doing here at this hour?" she asked, rubbing her eyes.

Dan took one look at her sleep-flushed face, her sensual lips, the tousled hair curling around her face, the sheer nightgown, and gulped. The ensemble left nothing to the imagination. "Never mind that," he growled. "Why in hell did you open the door?"

Was she hearing correctly? she wondered. Had he actually asked her why she had opened the door? She yawned. "Because you knocked on it and I didn't want to wake the neighbors. They might call the police." In her sleepy state, she collapsed against him, giving into a fit of silliness. "Get it?" She poked his ribs. "They might call the police. That's you. So you'd end up here, anyhow."

Dan was having a hard time keeping from laughing. He wanted to scoop her up in his arms, carry her back to her bedroom, and cover her with his hungry body. He almost did just that as she peered at him from beneath heavy lashes. She yawned again.

"It's the middle of the night," she said. "Is this some kind of a test? I saw your car from the window."

And he could see her nipples and every delectable inch of her. He swallowed hard. "Lesson number one, Millie. Never answer the door dressed like that. It would give a dead man the hots."

Millie glanced down at herself, then flung her arms in front of herself, covering her breasts. "Am I giving you the hots, Dan?" She lowered her eyelashes seductively, then yawned in his face. "Oops, sorry. Give me a minute."

Dan was grateful she left the room before she saw how obviously he wanted her. He recited the reasons that had brought him there. This wasn't going to work, he knew that with a sense of doom. He wanted her on a sheet; she wanted him on a sheet of paper.

A lousy trade-off, in his book.

*   *   *

"I'm ready." Millie, her eyelids still at half-mast, walked back into the room. One corner of her blouse was tucked into her jeans. She wore a pair of thongs. A pad and pencil dangled from her right hand.

"What's that for?" Dan asked, smiling in spite of himself. She looked adorable—and groggy.

She cupped her hand in front of her mouth, yawning once more. "In case anything happens. Notes."

He propelled her out the door, then took her key and locked up behind them. He steered her to the car and got her into it, making sure none of her was hanging out.

Praying for enormous self-control, he fastened her seat belt for her. His arms reaching across her, he closed his eyes and drew in a whiff of her perfume.

She reached up and tugged on the collar of his jacket. "Thank you, Dan. That was lovely."

Lovely. Only Millie would say buckling a seat belt was lovely. He smiled wryly. They were off on a stakeout where, if God was good to him, nothing would happen. He'd even arranged for a backup detail. His plan was simple. They'd stay an hour, then he'd bring her home. Between Millie's sleepiness and his libido, he was having a hard enough time trying to convince himself their relationship was all business.

His attempts at conversation elicited mostly short-tempered mumbles from her. After a while he gave up and simply drove in silence. With the big deal she and her agent had kicked up about wanting to see how a fascinating cop went about his fascinating business, he'd have thought the least she would do was stay awake.

He announced their arrival at their destination. She didn't answer. Glancing over, he wasn't surprised to see her fast asleep, her head listing to one side. A thick curtain of hair covered half her face. He gently nudged her upright. "We're here, sleeping beauty. Time to see how exciting this job is."

He expected her to ask a million questions and begin to fill up that pad of hers. Instead she mumbled a word approximating *wonderful*, scribbled something that looked unintelligible to him in her pad, then seemed to give up. She was out like a light. And no matter what he did, her head seemed to find its way onto his shoulder.

In the close confines of the car, her perfume was an exotic goad, setting his imagination alight. He remembered her as she'd opened the door, barefoot and standing in the light, clothed in a wisp of transparent white. "Oh, Millie," he muttered. "You really know how to play dirty pool."

Leaning over, he unbuckled her seat belt. His arm curved around her shoulders, drawing her close. "Don't hate me in the morning. I tried."

Like a contented kitten she curled into him, her hand lying innocently on his upper thigh. Her breasts flattened against his chest, proving undeniably that she wasn't wearing a bra.

In good conscience, he did try to move her hand,

only to have it flop back again. Beads of sweat broke out on his forehead. Millie's subconscious had a will of its own. She was touching him, teasing him, stoking the flames of his passion.

At this rate, he'd be a basket case by morning.

"What's a man to do?" he murmured, giving in to the irresistible urge to taste her creamy skin. His lips grazed her forehead, then drifted slowly to her soft cheek and the corner of her tantalizing mouth.

As if she'd slept in his arms a thousand times, she turned her face up, her lips seeking his. He felt as though he were caught in quicksand as he lowered his mouth to hers with the barest flutter of pressure. She murmured in her sleep. "Mmmm. . . . More."

He froze. What the hell was he doing, taking advantage of her? He knew all too well what he was doing and there was no excuse. He was behaving like a horny teenager. What made the whole thing impossible was that while he needed a cold shower, Millie was utterly unaware of what she had said, or even that she had touched him while she slept.

Very carefully, he lifted her hand. All right, Murdock, he told himself, don't go getting any fancy ideas. She wasn't responsible for her unconscious actions or reactions. She'd lived alone for a year. That had to be a tough adjustment. And you, Murdock, he reminded himself, are a chapter in a book to her, nothing more.

"Millie," he said, sitting her upright and speaking more sharply than he intended. "Wake up."

She did so slowly, like a flower unfolding. Her eyes, rimmed by those thick lashes, opened. At first she was disoriented, then she saw him and smiled. She stretched her arms upward, the action drawing her blouse taut against her breasts.

"Where are we?" she asked, regarding him with utmost trust. She didn't realize he was just this side of hell. "I'm sorry I catnapped, but it felt wonderful. I feel refreshed now, raring to go. Did anything exciting happen while I was asleep? Anything I should write down?"

He choked back a strangled groan.

"Not a thing, Millie," he lied, dampening his erotic urgency. "Not a thing."

She smiled at him, an innocent, sleep-refreshed smile. "That's good. I'd hate to miss anything."

Six

Dan hiked his knee into a more comfortable position. For the first time in an hour, he let his body relax. He'd been playing two ends against the middle. On the one hand he wanted to get to know Millie and have her get to know him, and on the other hand he was afraid to open old hurts lest it wound his family.

Millie awake was as curious as a cat. She badgered him with incisive, intelligent questions that kept him on track, kept him focusing on something other than the way her body had felt next to his.

Until Millie, his life had been uncomplicated and sane—if occasionally dangerous. He hadn't even felt the urge for a woman lately. He'd heard about men who burned out early. Read about it in her advice column, now that he thought about it.

America's most popular, most compelling romance novels...

Here, at last...love stories that really involve you!
Fresh, finely crafted novels with story lines so
believable you'll feel you're actually living them!
Characters you can relate to...exciting places to
visit...unexpected plot twists...all in all, exciting
romances that satisfy your mind and delight
your heart.

Millie was professional and serious, scribbling a mile a minute on her yellow lined pad. What would she do if he suddenly said, "Millie, I think you might be interested in knowing where your hand was while you were asleep. I can attest to the fact that you have the ability to arouse me in less than ten seconds. If you'd care to experiment while you're awake, we can replay the scene, including the part where you kissed me, then asked for more."

Millie touched his arm. "Dan, you aren't listening."

His patience straining, he told her to repeat the question.

"Do these crooks have priors?"

"Alleged perpetrators, Millie. Everyone's innocent until proven guilty." Himself included. "Yes, they do."

"And do you ever think about the danger?"

He wanted to shout that there was more danger being in a car with her than being out on the street. "I think about being prepared, not taking foolish chances. Cloning Rambo doesn't interest me." Unable to resist touching her any longer, he casually dropped a hand on her shoulder, rubbing the fabric of her blouse over her soft flesh.

Millie repressed a shiver of desire. Dan had no idea what he was doing to her. Yet she didn't want to move and possibly break the mood, not when he'd finally begun to talk about himself. "What interests you, Dan? Apart from the job, I mean?"

"Animal, vegetable, or mineral?"

She grinned. "Keep this up and I'll tell Wasach

he runs a boring precinct. He'll love that kind of publicity." Couldn't he tell how arousing his touch was? That his lightest caress could send the fires of passion flaring through her?

He smiled, abruptly sending her into thoughts of dark nights and silvery moonlight. "Be serious," she said. "Do you think of the danger?"

"From time to time. I am now," he said, twirling a lock of her hair around his finger. His eyes were level with hers as he leaned back to watch her. "Have you ever shot a gun, Millie?"

She could feel the tension build inside her. For the past hour her body had been reacting to him nonstop. She'd had letters from women telling her what had happened to them in cars, usually the backseat. She jerked herself back to his question.

"Only the ones at a shooting gallery on the boardwalk in Wildwood, New Jersey. I was trying to win a pink teddy bear."

"Did you?" he asked, remembering how intensely she'd concentrated on reeling in the fish. And how she'd used his body for support.

She pursed her lips. "No. It's very annoying. My brother says he inherited all the sharp-eyed genes and steady hands. It's a good thing, too. Kipp's a doctor. I can't hit the side of a barn."

He noted the disappointment. "I'll have to fix that."

She smiled brightly at him. She'd be able to use the information in her book, and maybe win the teddy bear the next time she was in Wildwood. It didn't matter that she could easily afford to buy one. She wanted just once in her life to pick off a prize with her skill. "You're going to take me to the shooting range and teach me how to shoot?"

Dan hated to dampen her spirits so soon after he'd lifted them. He liked this bubbly, carefree side of her. He leaned a bit closer. "No, I can't do that. That's for police personnel. But I can take you to some property I own up the coast. We'll set up some tin cans on the picket posts and see how you do." He frowned, surprised at how protective he felt toward her. "You really ought to take one of those self-defense courses. A woman should be able to defend herself. Men, too," he added, unwilling to reveal too much.

They were interrupted by a call from the dispatcher informing them of a robbery in progress. Millie immediately buckled her seat belt.

He put his hand over hers. "Sorry to disappoint you, Millie, but we're staying put. The call isn't for us." He checked his watch. His replacement would be along any minute. He reached under his seat, hauling up a thermos. "Have some," he said, unscrewing the top. "There are crackers in the glove compartment if you want."

She took the cup from him, placing a hand over the steaming brew as she stared out at the mostly deserted streets. It would be dawn in a few hours. Day Two. She was eating up her time with him.

"Murdock, you got me up in the middle of the night on a wild goose chase." She flapped the yellow pad at him. "You must admit this makes lousy copy. There's nothing to write about."

He almost choked on the hot coffee. "Not really.

You're seeing how a policeman exercises self-control and patience."

Millie gnawed on her bottom lip, thinking. She turned to a fresh sheet of paper, picked up her pencil, and fired off another charge. "I know being a policeman tends to run in families. Anyone in your family in the police force besides you?"

"No." His brows creased over disapproving eyes. He'd lulled himself into temporary amnesia over the real purpose of their being together. He'd talk with his father as soon as Dad and his mother returned from a trip abroad. If his father objected to any publicity that might dredge up his brother's name, he'd bow out of the arrangement.

"Was there?" she repeated.

"Let's keep it on me. Leave out the family tree."

"Dan," she protested, frowning. "I'd rather not. You're part of your family. The chapter will be bland. Why can't you understand and cooperate?" She'd hit a nerve. She knew it. Whom was he protecting?

Dan noted her high color, the intense way she was looking at him. Wanting to see how far she'd go for her story, he said, "Don't play detective. That's my job. You're the writer. That's your job. I'm sorry if you don't like coffee and crackers."

She backed off slightly, but not enough to keep the edge out of her voice. "How do you suggest we spend our time then? Gin rummy?"

She knew a brick wall when she hit one. Dan was perfectly amenable to having a companion help to pass the lonely hours in the car. He was perfectly willing to chat off the record. Yet the merest hint of on-the-record and he became a chameleon. Keep it general or keep it out.

Why? Was it because he resented having been forced into taking her in the first place? Was this how Murdock got even? Was there more?

She resolved to keep her cool. Ruffling his feathers wouldn't get her anywhere. But asking one of her computer whiz friends for some good, deep background on the Murdock family might give her something to go on.

"Can we at least talk off the record, Dan?"

His eyes narrowed fractionally. "Why? You can't use it."

"I want to know more about you," she answered honestly.

He sipped his coffee. His gaze rested on her lips, then flicked upward. "Do I get to ask questions, too?"

She smiled, thinking, You're not going to get away that easily, my friend. "Of course, when I'm through."

"No ladies first?" he teased.

"No one is interested in the private Millie Gordon. The public knows what it needs to about my other persona, Ms. M."

Intrigued, Dan pushed further. "I'm not your public."

"Dan, this is ridiculous."

"I totally agree. When two grown people who are obviously attracted to each other have to set down rules for discussion, it is ridiculous."

Millie was building herself up to a full-blown fit

of indignation. "Who said we're attracted to each other?"

He kissed her quickly, surprising her. Her lips parted in semi-automatic shock, and he took advantage of the opportunity. He kissed her deeply, sending her into a hot, heady spiral. When he broke away, she was breathing heavily, but he seemed totally unaffected.

"Our bodies are way ahead of our conversation," he said. "And they're a lot more honest."

His voice seemed so bland to her, he might have been talking about the weather, Millie thought. Well, she could be blasé, too.

"The only thing I want is a good story," she said, mentally crossing her fingers. "Something that will make the readers not want to read that last word on my last line."

"Are you sure? I believe in honesty, too. Let's see if I can convince you that what's between us is important enough to keep out of print."

His lips moved over hers in savage, sensual domination. She hadn't a chance; he knew how to arouse her. They'd been close in a car before. Their bodies were attuned, and fit together perfectly. She felt her resistance melt just as he dragged his mouth from hers.

She surfaced, still tasting him on her lips, still feeling his hard chest muscles. She gazed into his blackguard eyes, reading in them hot desire and certain he could gloat over what he read in hers.

She shivered, not from the cool night but from the heat radiating from him. Oh, he was clever. She gave him that. If she agreed to confidentiality, he boxed her in. He could spill his guts out and ethically she couldn't use the material. His fingers traced circles on her bare arm, making it difficult for her to concentrate. He looked incredibly calm and controlled and about as guileless as a mountain fox.

How would she explain this to Wylie?

"Millie, I never said I was a suitable subject for your book. Your agent and Wasach cooked that up."

"You're saying this deliberately to discourage me."

His smile almost reached his eyes. "I'm a very deliberate man."

His hand traveled up to her cheek and caressed her. She swallowed. She wanted—needed—to know more about him. So she gambled. "All right. You have my promise. Off the record tonight. Tomorrow, that deal's off."

"Fair enough. Thank you." His hand glided around to the back of her neck, drawing her closer. "I appreciate that."

"Do you ever lose, Dan?" She'd been finessed and trapped by his smooth talk and her own treacherous body.

He smoothed the hair away from her brow. "Sure. Mostly when I don't particularly care about the stakes." He wondered at what point he'd decided, as far as Millie was concerned, to throw years of caution to the winds. "Do you get the impression," he asked softly, "that putting us in a car together is dangerous?"

"You could shake my hand," she whispered.

Bare inches separated them. "Uh-uh. I like this better."

"You know, don't you?" she said weakly. "I can't write about this."

He chuckled. "I know, but this is a lot more fun than answering questions. Did anyone ever tell you those eyes of yours are an extraordinary shade of blue?" He kissed those eyes shut, a soft murmur escaping her lips.

"Dan," she managed to say, forcing away a swift stab of desire, "you're on duty."

His lips brushed her forehead. "Not anymore. There's an unmarked car about thirty-five feet behind us. He's my relief. He's been here for the last ten minutes. Don't worry—he didn't see us kiss."

Infuriated, she gave a mighty push against his chest. She might have known he'd be in perfect physical condition. "You sneak. You went through all this to prevent me from questioning you."

He laughed and kissed the tip of her nose. "I went through all this, as you put it, to see if I can be in a car with you without kissing you. I can't."

Then he stopped talking, blocking out the world for her as he had in the past. She had a strong sense of déjà vu, as if her body were reliving an earlier scene, a scene of soft mists and sensations and heat.

A wild, passionate force erupted within her. Dan's tongue teased and tempted hers. His lips were firm and commanding, yet soft and beckoning. Later, she would wonder why she hadn't had the desire to push him away. Why she had let herself be kissed like a teenager.

She would wonder why she had allowed his lips to devour hers, his tongue to pillage her mouth. Why his kissing her seemed so right, so natural, so familiar. She would also ask herself why her arms had encircled his neck and her fingers had threaded through his thick hair while he pressed his body to hers; ask herself how an otherwise sensible woman who knew the score could let herself in for such trouble. Trouble she didn't need, but which she seemed to court whenever she and Dan were within seat belt distance.

Gradually Dan pulled away, his lips lingering on hers for a moment longer before he moved back to his side of the car. Millie felt twinges of both disappointment and relief. She hadn't wanted him to stop. If he'd continued, though, she knew she'd probably have had some firsthand experience about what could happen in the backseat of a car.

"Definitely off limits," Dan muttered to himself, reaffirming his convictions about being in a car with Millie. He stuck the key into the ignition. "I'd better get you home. We have a heavy day tomorrow."

Millie blinked. She was still feeling aftershocks. He'd silenced her questions with the oldest trick in the book. Male to female. She'd fallen into his arms without a struggle, agreeing to everything he'd asked.

Dan pulled out into the road, signaling to the man in the car behind him. He glanced over at

Millie; he wanted to tell her the truth, but knew he had no right to tell her the whole story about Jack Murdock. Not without going against his father's wishes.

"What . . ." Millie started, then paused to clear her throat. "What's this about tomorrow?"

"Oh, we're going to a game."

"What game?" She stared at him without comprehension.

"Softball. How good are you at catching?"

Was he crazy? She had work to do. Tomorrow, as far as she was concerned, was Day Two. She already knew the score: Dan two; Millie zero.

Ben stepped into Dan's office. It was eight in the morning. "Geez, you look like hell. What happened last night?"

Dan looked up. His eyes were strained from the mountain of paperwork on his desk. He hadn't slept all night. Millie had gotten into his blood like a fever.

"Dammit, Ben. Wear shoes I can hear, or else knock. Nothing exciting happened. Mike made the collar after we left last night."

Ben slipped into the empty chair in front of Dan's desk. "Then why are you so grumpy?"

"I'm not grumpy. I'm busy." He tapped his pen on the edge of the desk. "Don't you have paperwork to do, too?"

"Yeah, but I'm not hyper about it."

Ben stretched his long legs in front of him. He was completely relaxed. "What's ticking you off today? You act as if you have a burr under your saddle. How come? Louie's still being a good boy. Aren't you and Millie getting along all right?"

Dan's spirits had plummeted with each hour that passed since he'd dropped Millie off at her house. He was in over his head and he didn't like it. The problem was he and Millie could be getting along famously—provided he gave her what she wanted.

"Sorry, Ben. I was thinking about my dad's brother. I'm trying to figure out why Uncle Jack turned into a bad cop. He was my idol when I was a kid. Finding out he had such feet of clay really hurt."

Ben shrugged. "Who can say what's in another man's head? Things happen. Pressures build. You're not responsible."

"Yeah, maybe so, but I have a clear memory of what it did to the family. It nearly killed my dad. It took him years to work out his shame. He idolized his older brother."

"So that's what's bugging you. You're afraid this book Millie's writing will trigger old memories and reopen old wounds for your dad. And yourself, looks like . . . ?"

Dan rustled a sheaf of papers. "Something like that. Wasach sees me as the great white hope to force the city council fathers to buy us the equipment we need. Hell of a fix I'm in." He smiled grimly. "I never thought I'd live to see the day Pete would use me as a bargaining chip."

Ben unfolded a paper clip and traced its design

on paper with his pen. "You could refuse. Or you could take Millie into your confidence."

Dan had considered that at about four A.M., but discarded the idea. There would be no reason for them to be together otherwise. He was pretty sure after his machismo display in the car that she'd say no to a date.

"I can't tell Millie yet," he said. "I figure I'll play this out for a few more days. She's promised me the right to edit anything I don't like."

Ben dropped the clip into an ashtray. "Seems to me that's a pretty unusual concession. Most writers would be irritated as hell at being censored."

"I told her I wouldn't agree otherwise."

Ben nodded as he stood up. "Are we still on for the softball game? The little pumpkin said she can play today if you need another man. That is, if you're still planning on meeting the guys."

Dan leaned back, lacing his fingers behind his head. "Haven't missed a game yet, have I? Ben, do me a favor, will you?"

"What?"

"Call her Natalie and take a good look at her. She's no man. She's got legs and breasts and a cute little rump."

Ben looked affronted, as if he'd just been accused of not knowing the difference between men and women. "Is Millie going, too?"

Dan shook his head. His friend was as blind as a bat where Natalie was concerned. "Millie's going. The agreement was one week."

Ben's smile crinkled his eyes. "Well, cheer up. You have only five more days after today."

The implication that he wouldn't be seeing Millie after five days made Dan wonder exactly what he did want. All he knew was that he hadn't slept well in two nights for thinking about her. He'd be a zombie by the end of the week.

Ben paused at the door, his hand on the knob. "Dan, is it wise, bringing Millie to a game with your group? Suppose something triggers one of them off? You'd have a gang riot on your hands."

"Quit sounding like a mother hen. The guys have made progress. They've got jobs and are contributing to society." His monthly game with the team was important. They depended on him. It had taken a long time to build their trust. "I'll handle it."

"Just so you know what you're doing."

Dan recognized the note of warning in Ben's voice. "I told you, I'll keep them in line. Besides, nothing's going to happen."

"You always were a softie."

"Bull. I'm the guy who arrested them and put them inside."

Millie took a red pen and crossed off yesterday's date on the calendar. Today, she'd bring her tape recorder and wouldn't let Dan off the hook so easily.

She walked out onto the patio. The sky was a bright blue with high cirrus clouds. The water in the canal was calm. The fishing boats had already left. A few people were sitting on their patios enjoying the cool morning air. The weatherman predicted another hot day.

Henry and Henrietta sat on the grass, their necks curved downward. When they saw her they rose majestically, like two statues coming to life.

"Good morning, you two. Guess what? Millie's going to make a fool of herself today. If she's very lucky she won't fall on her face!"

She was wiping the slate clean, she decided as she fed the birds. Yesterday never happened. Today she'd add to her store of information.

She did her stretching exercises, then walked back into the house to dress. Considering the weather forecast and that she'd be playing ball, she dressed in shorts and a cropped cotton top.

When she saw Dan drive up, she hurried to the door, determined not to show by expression or deed that last night meant something to her.

Smiling, she flung open the door. "Hello, Dan."

A long breath escaped him when he saw her fire-engine red shorts, a matching red shirt, dangling red earrings, and sneakers. Her hair was tied up in a pony tail. She could have been an ad for the all-American girl. All wrong.

"Millie, you look terrific. Now will you please change your clothes." He spoke calmly, but there was no mistaking the steel behind his tone.

Color stained her cheeks as her quick anger flared. She lifted her chin in defiance. "Why?"

His shoulders moved eloquently. "Because we're going to be playing ball with a bunch of men."

"I hadn't thought we'd be playing with a bunch of geese," she said huffily.

"Very funny. Please change your clothes. You're half naked. Suppose you fall?" he said, grasping at straws. She'd have his men at each other's throats.

"If I fall, I'll pick myself up."

"Millie, the team is made up of ex-cons."

"Ex-cons?" she repeated, her writer's instincts smelling a story. "Why are you playing with ex-cons?"

"They've served their time and are trying to go straight. We play once a month, mostly so I can stay in touch with them."

Intrigued by this information, she asked, "How do you know them?"

He looked past her to a point on the wall. "I was the one who arrested them."

Now that was something she could use in her book. "And you play ball with them? How'd you manage that?"

For the first time since she'd met him, he seemed genuinely embarrassed. "Someone has to give them a chance to change. The jails are too crowded." His gaze roamed over her scantily clad body. "Can't you be comfortable in pants and a long-sleeved shirt? I'm not trying to tempt the fates here."

He was standing very close to her, so close that she felt an urgent need to ask a question. "If we weren't playing with ex-cons, would you be asking me to wear something else?"

His hand tarried with a lock of her hair. "Would you want me to?"

She felt the thudding of her heart, the electricity between them. She tilted her head to one side, gazing into his fathomless gray eyes.

He had the face of a Greek god—carved in granite, softened only when he smiled. Strength and tenderness were both there, doled out judiciously.

He'd obviously just showered and shaved. His hair was damp and she caught the waft of his cologne. He wore a pair of faded denim cotton shorts and a matching polo shirt. There was no use denying the attraction she felt toward him. They'd been headed down this path since they'd met.

She realized that he'd answered her question with a question. Ignoring the voice of reason, she twined her arms around his neck. Instantly she was lost in a golden haze. His mouth was the sun and she was reaching for its warmth.

She wanted him to kiss her. The pounding of his heart matched hers. Last night hadn't been a mistake. There was a fire in her blood. When he drew her into his arms and held her tight, she no longer cared why she was there, only that she was.

"Oh, Millie." He buried his lips in her hair. "I want you."

He trailed kisses along her neck and face and felt her quiver. She was where he wanted her to be. He kissed her leisurely, saying hello with his lips and hands. When his fingers cupped her breast, feeling the nipples harden, he cursed the time. Kissing her tenderly, he took her on a trembling journey. He didn't press, he didn't demand, but rather let her show him what she wanted of him.

"I want you," he repeated.

His words penetrated her foggy brain. Want was easier than need. Want was a casual excuse for an affair. She wanted everything. She wanted nothing. She was confused by her own actions. She tore her lips from his. Her chest rose and fell with her rapid breaths.

He let her go reluctantly. His breath came out on a sigh as ragged as hers. He pressed a kiss to her palm, then kissed her lightly on the mouth.

"It seems," he murmured, "an automobile isn't the only place that's dangerous for us to be alone. Change your clothes, Millie. We're late."

Seven

Murdock's Maniacs was made up of ex-juvenile delinquents who would have been in and out of jail if it weren't for Dan. They voted to make Millie the umpire, and then explained the rules of the game to her. She flipped the Maniacs' cap backward and offered her first official speech as umpire. "Piece of cake," she said, patting two hulking players on the back. "Let the best man win. Play ball."

Dan rolled his eyes heavenward. The men stared at her for a moment, then laughed themselves silly. The ice was broken.

Dan had been a bit apprehensive about bringing Millie after Ben's words of caution. The men hailed from a tough street world where distrust was the name of the game. But Millie breezed into their midst, behaving as if she'd met his motley crew when they were in the church choir. By seeking their help with the rudiments of the game, she broke down their initial barriers. By the bottom of the second, the entire team was eating out of her hand.

Millie gave Dan a little flak when she first spied Natalie Gershon as they arrived at the field.

"She's wearing shorts!" Millie exclaimed. "Why aren't you telling her what to wear? Do you realize the humidity's awful?"

"Natalie," he patiently explained, "can take care of herself. Besides, these guys aren't about to get involved with a cop. She could drop-kick any one of them and they know it. You're different." *And you're mine*, he thought, knowing he had no right to tell her that.

Millie glanced down at herself. At least she had gotten Dan to compromise on a short-sleeved shirt. "I'm different all right. I'm the one who's going to roast. Long pants. Hah."

By the top of the seventh Dan's team was trailing by a score of four to three. Dan was at bat. Joe Moreno, displaying the same grace and fluid motion he used to strip a car in three minutes flat, was on the pitcher's mound, peering straight at the catcher. Behind Dan, Tony Graham crouched down, signaling the play with a variation of the code he had used to alert his gang when the cops approached. Joe nodded in answer to the call, reached back, and let go. In the past, his pitch had been clocked at seventy miles an hour.

Dan, with two strikes against him, swung with all his might, his arm, shoulder, and back muscles straining through the delivery. The ball was on its way deep into left field.

Millie silently rooted for him. She knew Dan was doing something with and for these young men besides having fun. He was their role model. They treated him with respect and affection. She pulled the cap off her head and wondered if he'd ever been simply a story to her, or if she'd always been most interested in him as a man.

Dan ran full steam to first base, rounded the corner, took the signal from Natalie, and kept going, his powerful legs pumping hard. In left field Whitey Kane, an ex-cat burglar, scooped up the ball. He threw it to Frank Gargan at second, who caught it on a fast dive just as Dan slid into base.

Flushed with success, Dan stood up, wiped the sweat from his face, and grinned. It was the best play he'd made all afternoon. Excited, he clapped Frank on the back.

"Too bad, Frank. Those are the breaks."

He looked over to Millie to see if she would congratulate him. He figured he'd earned her accolade. And there she was, sprinting toward him. She opened her arms wide—and hugged Frank. Who happily hugged her back.

"You're out, Dan," she said. "Frank's toe was on the bag first. Great play, Frank."

Dan couldn't believe his ears. "I was safe!" he stormed.

"Too bad, man," Frank said. "Those are the breaks." He doubled over with glee.

Millie smiled graciously, as befitted a woman

whose word was law. The urge to kiss her was nearly overwhelming, but Dan managed to turn and stalk to the fence where the rest of his team was standing.

The inning continued. Dan watched as Millie trotted to the pitcher's mound in her self-appointed roles as coach and Mother Superior. Joe's last pitch had been off his stride and he was visibly upset. Disgruntled, Dan saw her turn on the charm. Jealousy was a new emotion for him. He soundlessly mimicked her words to Joe.

"You're terrific, Joe. Ease up just a bit and show me what you've got."

She swung around, grazing Dan with a broad wink. He laughed in spite of himself. He meant to ask her later exactly how long she had been playing softball. Millie clearly operated on her own agenda.

Dan was up again in the eighth inning. In another close play, this time at first, Millie called him out. The Maniacs loved it.

"You're going to make the men think I'm a pansy," he growled in her ear. He desperately wanted to kiss her.

She tweaked his nose. He was sweaty, mean, tough, and oh, so handsome. "Well, Murdock, I can personally attest to the fact you're no sissy. Want me to put that in my book? You'll get all the women after you."

She had miscalculated the effect of her words. He grabbed her and kissed her full on the mouth in front of everyone, locking her in a vise with his arms. Catcalls and whistles cheered him on.

He lifted his head. "Write whatever the hell you want."

The blood was pounding in Millie's head. She drew back until her gaze locked with his. His eyes were flecked with tiny specks of green; his hair danced as he ran his fingers through it. He had the superior look of a man thoroughly pleased with himself. In two days he'd succeeded in keeping her totally off balance.

"Batter up, men," she called, a little shakily. "Murdock's insane."

He kissed her quickly. "You got that right, toots."

The game ended in a tie. Normally they played until there was a winner, but Dan saw Millie flagging from the heat. He spoke to a few of the players and Phil, a seventeen-year-old who played first base, walked over to Millie.

"We're bushed," he said, "and we want ice cream. Do you mind if we quit?"

Millie's shirt was sticking to her. She was hot and tired and thirsty. "Let's go."

The owner of the ice-cream parlor knew Dan and the others. Ben and Natalie split up, each sitting with a different group. Millie immediately realized they were helping Dan. He moved from table to table, spending time with each group. If it appeared one of the men needed to talk, another would get up to make room for Dan.

Millie turned to Joe, sitting beside her in the booth. "What do you think of Dan?"

"He's the best," Joe said instantly. "I hated cops before I met him. And I used to strip cars. That's how Dan found me. Man, I hated that dude back then." Joe slurped the remainder of his chocolate float, poking his spoon to get the last drops. He licked the chocolate off the spoon. "My ma blesses him now."

"What changed your mind about him?"

He shot her an amazed look. "How many cops vouch for you after they arrest you? Dan showed up every day. I still didn't trust him. He was there at the trial. He came to see me regularly, droning it into my head about finishing high school and making something of myself. The guy was a real pest. He'd show up with my mother. She'd say how proud she was of me. . . ." Joe shook his head in wonder.

"I can see why," Millie said. Heroes come in many packages and guises. Dan was a hero. This was her opening hook for her first chapter.

Joe dangled his spoon. "Imagine, my own mother saying she was proud of me. And I was in jail. How could I let her and Dan down? My old man wasn't around."

Pride and bitterness, Millie thought. Bitterness for an absent father. Pride in himself because someone cared. Because of Dan, a mother had found pride in a son. And a son had found pride in his difficult manhood. "What are you doing now, Joe?"

"Dan fixed it so I can go to junior college. I'm doing okay. I'm going on to get my degree." He looked at her with shining dark eyes. "No one in my family ever went to college. But I want to be an electrical engineer."

She put one hand on his arm. "You've got success written all over you, Joe." When he blushed, she asked, "Do you have a girlfriend?"

"There is someone I like. It's not like you and Dan, though."

Millie gasped. She realized that with his kiss, Dan had laid claim to her in front of everyone.

"What's this big lug saying?" Dan asked, slipping into the booth. He draped his arm around her shoulders.

"Oh, nothing," she said. "We were just shooting the breeze."

For the next few minutes Dan and Joe chatted while Millie listened. Dan didn't preach, didn't lecture, but instead posed thoughtful suggestions. When they were alone in the car returning to her home, she was quiet.

"Penny for your thoughts, Millie?"

"I'm thinking," she said seriously, "that I haven't even scratched the surface of knowing you."

"For your book?"

"For me." The truth slipped out so easily, it astounded her.

He squeezed her hand. "That's easily remedied. I think it's time I showed you how the other half lived."

"Where are we going?"

His gaze locked with hers. "To my house."

"Do you live near here?" she asked, aware of how her heartbeat had speeded up.

"Not too far. We're almost there."

She told herself that seeing his home was important to the story. They could be good friends. She'd be going home to New Jersey soon where she belonged and the time with Dan would be a pleasant memory. She leaned back in her seat and spent the rest of the drive trying to convince herself her lies were the truth.

A charming, relatively old Victorian-style, his house was situated in a neighborhood with stately palmetto palms planted thirty years ago or so, when the houses were almost new. Latticework surrounded a wide veranda dotted with blue wicker rockers. The extended roofline shaded the porch from the hot sun. Hibiscus bushes intermixed with succulents created a natural border along the stone pathway.

"What a lovely house," she said sincerely.

Dan smiled. He wanted her to like his home. He wanted to see her in every room of it. He wanted to be able to breathe her scent and remember her in the cool of the night when he needed her most.

"Thanks," he said. "I like it." He linked his hand with hers. "I'll show you around."

"How rude would I be if I asked to use the shower first?"

"Can I come too?" he teased.

They showered separately. Millie had brought a change of clothing with her, another bright red blouse and a softly flowing white cotton skirt. She and Dan met up again in the large, cool living room.

"The furniture is comfortably old," he said as she toured the room. "Someday I'll toss it and get new stuff. This is mostly hand-me-downs from family. I think they used me as a replacement for the Salvation Army. It never mattered before." The implication that it mattered now sent her emotions into a tailspin.

The room featured a gold Lawson sofa, a well-used leather recliner, several overstuffed chairs, a standing lamp, and two end tables with attached lamps. Good, serviceable furniture for a bachelor who didn't particularly care about décor. She caught herself seeing the home as it might be, bright and cheerful in light, airy colors.

"Do you play?" she asked, walking over to the upright piano in one corner.

"I tickle the ivories once in a while," he admitted. "How about you?"

It was a house for a family, she thought. A family and music. "A little." In fact, she played very well. She missed her Baldwin.

"Why don't you try it?" he suggested. "See if it needs tuning."

"Maybe later." She hadn't touched a piano since Frank's death. Had it really been more than a year? And was she really standing in another man's house thinking about wanting him to make love with her?

The shadow was there, fleeting and sad. Dan saw it and wondered. He led her into the dining room. There was an oval oak table and six high-backed chairs. A crystal chandelier hung above a silver candelabra centerpiece.

"Your family gave you very nice hand-me-downs," she said.

"Maybe they're trying to tell me something. What do you think?" he asked quietly.

She tensed. "Probably. Parents usually get over-excited on the subject of marriage and carrying on the family name."

"And you, Millie? What do you think?"

"I think," she said, feeling the heat as his gaze blatantly caressed her, lingering on her breasts, "that it's none of my business." She moistened her lips and stared at the silver candelabra. "You have this nasty habit of doing all the questioning, Dan. I often ask myself why."

"And what answer do you get?"

She flipped on the light, studying the prisms in the chandelier. "None. You're not a man who opens up easily."

He couldn't just yet. They went into his study. The well-used room beckoned to her. She wanted to ask about the wall of bookshelves crammed with books, but didn't.

Dan walked over to the stereo and turned it on, filling the room with the sublime strains of Mozart. He turned back to Millie. The light streaming in at the window glowed on her shiny hair. She belongs in a room like this, Dan thought. A room of quiet beauty and passion.

"Dan, why did you quit law school?"

He picked up a paperweight, palming it from hand to hand. "I needed more money. At the time, I was married and attending school on a double-track program."

"Double track?"

"A double-track program allows you to take the same subject in the daytime or the evening, your choice. Not many schools offer it. But the truth is, I was restless."

Millie understood the feeling. She was filled with restlessness herself. She wanted to move across to him, to touch him. She remained perfectly still.

"I'd sit in class," he went on, "listen to the lecture, then go home to pore over books or work my shift. I began to wonder why I was there. I envied the others who knew they wanted to join the best law firm in town and make gobs of money. There wasn't a ladder most weren't ready to climb in the pursuit of the American dream. Money, not law, was the real ambition. I kept thinking life should be more meaningful, more exciting."

Would he always choose a life of dodging bullets? she wondered, sitting down on the couch. She couldn't bear the possibility of his getting hurt. "But what if you want to resume your studies?"

Fate and circumstances, he thought. It all boiled down to that. His had altered in the last week, irrevocably, from the day he'd met her. "If I choose to do so, I can return. If the reason were compelling."

Tiny darts of excitement radiated from the base of her stomach to her throat. She needed to uncover the real Dan Murdock. She needed . . .

"Dan, did you quit school because of your wife?" She saw him stiffen and knew she'd touched another raw nerve. What else was in his past?

He joined her on the couch, crossing his long legs. "This is off the record, Millie.

"I was a few years older than Lana. We started dating when I was in college and she was in high school. I was brought up in an old-fashioned way, where the boy picked the girl up at her home.

Lana always found an excuse to meet me several blocks from her house, though. In those days I didn't recognize the signs of child abuse.

"Her mother had died when she was twelve, leaving her the burden of the housework. One day—she was out of school and working as a clerk in a department store and I was a senior—I was late for a date. She wasn't where we usually met, so I went to her house."

Dan grimaced. Millie felt his temper as he continued. "Her father was drunk, mean, ugly, vicious drunk. Lana didn't want me to see what the bastard had done to her. He'd beaten her. Her eyes were swollen, her lips cut, her face blotchy.

"I wish I had known. She always wore long-sleeved dresses or blouses, even in hot weather. I never knew."

He stared across the room. "I brought her to my parents' home. Her father was so drunk he didn't miss her or even try to find her for three days. Mom and Dad took Lana in to live with us. We had enough cops in the family to scare the life out of her father. My . . . my Uncle Jack threatened to beat her father up if he came near her."

Millie saw his face tighten as he stumbled over his uncle's name. She sensed there was something he wasn't telling her. The reporter in her filed away the name.

"I graduated from college," Dan continued, "joined the police force, and enrolled in law school. It was an ambitious plan. Dad was retiring early. He had put his time in. Before he started a new career he and Mom wanted to travel. Lana and I eloped."

"Did you love her very much?"

He stood up and walked over to the window, cramming his hands in his pockets. "I cared for her, but after she came to live with us, both our feelings changed. We were more like brother and sister. The marriage was doomed from the start. Our intentions were good. We were just too young.

"We kept the marriage alive while I helped her through college. She's remarried now. She's happy and even has a good job. Makes a hell of a story, doesn't it?"

Millie had dug her nails into her palms to keep from interrupting. Now she rose. She crossed the room to Dan and put her arms around his waist, hugging him. Her head rested against his strong back. He'd taken on so many burdens with that back, she thought. Yet he hurt. Tears filled her eyes for the young man who had bravely tried to right the ills of the world. He'd given her a precious gift with his trust.

Dan felt drained but strangely at peace. At Millie's touch his rigidly held body relaxed. He'd never told another woman the details of his youthful marriage. He curled his hands over hers and pulled her around in front of him.

Droplets of unshed tears moistened her thick lashes. He studied her face, seeing the sadness and the longing there. He knew she wasn't even aware of her longing. It clung to her, as it clung to him. Like him, she had needs. They'd both been denied too long.

"Millie, don't cry," he whispered.

She wiped her eyes with her hand. "I'm fine, really. I won't use the information, but shouldn't we be formalizing this interview? I'll get my pad and pencil."

"Should we?" he asked. "Do you really want to ask me a bunch more?"

The expression in his eyes should have warned her, as should the huskiness in his voice. The musky scent of sexual heat should have warned her that to start with this man meant hitching a ride to his extravagant star.

He touched her with nothing save his eyes—those smoky, intense gray eyes—yet she felt his brand on every part of her body. In her lonely heart and aching breasts, in her most secret places. Wherever his gaze touched, she blazed.

"Wouldn't you rather see where this heat takes us first, Millie?"

Her mind, that safe control center that had served her well until now, shut down as needs stronger than she'd ever felt before tore through her. A part of her cried for what might have been, cried for the young Dan, just as that long-dormant part of her begged for release with the mature man he had become. She felt rooted to the spot, powerless to deny the hunger she read in his eyes.

He brushed his lips across hers. "Tell me you want me as much as I want you."

She did want this man, shamelessly. Now. She barely breathed. . . . "Yes."

What he read in her jewellike eyes filled him

with tenderness. He bent down, grazing her lips in a butterfly kiss. Then another and another, until both strained for more.

He lifted his head and smiled. His gentleness was her undoing. She pressed her body closer to his, sliding her hands up over his shoulders. He felt so good, so strong, so very much alive. She marveled at the hard muscle alive under her eagerly probing fingers.

Pivoting her, he held her against him, her back to his front. He slipped his hands around her slim waist, his fingers pointing downward.

"Since the first moment in the car, I knew I wanted you," he said with quiet intensity. He dipped his head to kiss the soft flesh below her ear. "We'll have each other," he vowed. "We'll make it beautiful."

His touch robbed her of breath. His promise of beauty was like a benediction. She spread her hands over his, moving to his rhythm. He was hard and strong and infinitely tender.

Moaning, she nestled her head back, cushioning it in the curve of his shoulder. She watched, almost mesmerized, as together their hands gently squeezed her belly. Just as hypnotically, he stoked the flames inside her, fanning them into a fiery blaze. Murmuring endearments to her, he spread rampaging embers to every fiber of her being.

She turned and kissed him hungrily. Her passionate response delighted him. He had known this was in her. With Millie pressed tightly to him, he rotated his hips.

"See how much I want you?" he murmured.

"Millie, you did this. You have this power over me."

His hands moved upward, feeling and knowing her as a blind man would learn a delicate flower. Her breasts filled his palms, blossoming in his hands.

"I want to look at you, Millie." Her blue eyes shone with absolute trust. Exhilarated by it, he unbuttoned her blouse.

She felt his fingers brush her skin. One button . . . two . . . three. . . . A cool rush of air touched her breasts. Blouse and bra slipped off her shoulders, and Dan looked at her with adoration. "So beautiful."

He bent his head to kiss her. His tongue laved first one nipple, then the other. Whatever he touched, he caressed reverently. He has the soul of a poet, she thought. It seemed the most natural act in the world to hold his head against her. She exalted in his mouth sucking first one breast and then the other. The sucking motion tugged deep— between her thighs she felt a readying moisture. She bent over him, her hair curtaining them in hedonistic privacy.

Sensations flowed through her and raced through him.

Sensual, stimulating, stirring.

He felt them all as he drank of her sweetness. "Ah, Millie. You're magnificent. Let me show you how I want to love you."

He was asking for permission to continue. Again his gentleness stirred her. Life called to life, helping her shed the past. "Yes," she whispered.

He pulled off his shirt. Flesh met flesh and they gasped in delight. This first time. This special time.

Smiling into each other's eyes, they stood pressed together. Neither wanted to hurry. They rejoiced in the sensual gratifications of giving and taking.

Their lips touched. Sweetly. Playfully. Love bites. Soft laughter.

So many delicious places to kiss, she thought. Like the corner of his mouth. "Rough beard."

"I should have shaved."

"No, don't. I like you this way."

"I'll grow a beard, then."

"Silly."

He lingered over her soft cheek, then closed her eyes with tender kisses. "Bluer than the deepest ocean," he said into her hair.

"There's a song there, Dan."

"We'll compose it together. You be the bass. I'll be the high notes."

"Dopey, it's the other way around."

He laughed. "I never knew. Your perfume is driving me wild."

"Really?"

"Really."

"I'll douse myself with it."

"Will you let me put it on you?"

She smiled. "If you like."

"You should have candles, Millie. Scented white candles circling a bed, with a mirror on the ceiling, and a feather boa across your breasts for me to . . ."

"To what?"

He kissed the teasing smile from her face. "I don't know. I'll think of something."

She was sure he would. "And what do I do?"

"You lie there and let me play." His mouth on hers, he sent his tongue on an erotic journey that left them both breathless.

She knew she was more than a little infatuated with him. Neither could yet say the word of commitment—love.

"I've known you forever," he whispered.

"A lifetime in a few days."

The hair on his chest was silky soft. She ran her fingers through it, then kissed his nipples as he'd kissed hers.

"More than enough time." A glint of humor lit his eyes. "We'll keep this off the record, too."

She rained kisses on his face and neck, then suggestively thrust her hips forward. "Mmm, my pleasure."

She touched his lips, tracing their outline with her tongue.

"Oh, Lord," he said, then groaned. His hands framed her face. The silver in his eyes had darkened to gray-black. "I've never wanted a woman as much as I want you. This kiss will be our first, Millie. The others were just practice."

She steeped herself in his scent. The misery of the recent past slipped from her shoulders. Only the present counted. She wouldn't think about the tomorrows when she'd no longer be there, when her vacation must end. "More. Now," she cried urgently, letting the words tumble into his mouth.

"Now," he breathed into hers, cupping her buttocks.

His tongue slipped into her mouth, and like a flower she opened to welcome him. They had waited almost too long. The heat was almost too scorching. Their bodies sought each other with an intensity that threatened to engulf them.

He'd promised her memories. She knew she would at least have them.

He kissed her wildly, ecstasy flowing from his inflamed loins to hers, heightening the tensions screaming for release. When he lifted his head, breaking their sustained kiss, his ragged breathing matched hers.

Touching, tasting, neither could say whose heart beat faster. Eyes glazed with passion, he held her close to his side as he led her toward the bedroom. The bed was large and masculine, like its owner. The room held the mementos of a man very different from her husband.

He felt her tremble and temporary panic shot through him. Taking her face in his hands, he looked directly into her eyes. "Millie, don't you want this, too?"

How could she tell him that for all the advice she'd given to women all over the country, ultimately nothing counted for her? She was, she realized, frightened. "There's been no one except my husband," she whispered.

He understood. Millie was vulnerable. "Then you make me very proud. I hope I'll please you."

"Please me?" she repeated in wonder, some of her doubts flowing away from her. "Dan, you—"

"Shh, no more talk."

He stripped off his clothes, then reverently undressed her, kissing each exposed part of her body as her clothes drifted to the floor. "Come here, beautiful." He curved his hand around her nape, drawing her fully against him.

She was sent whirling by the bold touch of his body, his lips seeking hers. It stamped forever a different brand on her psyche. The gentleness he'd shown until now was replaced by white hot passion. He made love to her with his mouth on hers; with his hands stroking her body's pleasure points; with erotic words of love hoarsely whispered.

Desire made him taut as a wire. Need made him hold back. For the first time in his adult life he was as vulnerable as the woman who'd entrusted him with the gift of herself. He was in danger of losing his mind, and, if he weren't very careful, his heart.

He bent to take a nipple in his mouth, teasing it, laving it with pleasure. When she thought she could stand no more, he laughed, then did the same to the other. Her breasts became the center of her being, jolting long-dormant nerve centers into raging life.

She slid her hands up his arms and across his wide shoulders, exploring and charting the muscles underlying his smooth skin. Her fingers curled through his hair. She pulled his face to hers, kissing him until she heard him moan.

Hunger matched desire, driving them both. Millie felt suspended above herself, tossed up in a storm, whirling in its vortex. Dan lifted her onto the bed, and she gasped at the intense heat of his body as he lay on top of her.

He kissed her with a savagery of want. He took all she had, adoring her body as one would pray at a shrine. His fingers found the moist, hot center of her, and he knew she wanted him as much as he wanted her.

"Look at me." His voice was rough. He wanted to watch the miracle of her as he entered her.

She smiled up at him, her blue eyes smoky with passion. "I know," she whispered.

A groan ripped from him as she lifted her hips. He came into her then, and she arched against him, taking him fully. He carried her higher than she had ever been. He made love to her with a raw, primitive force with jungle heat.

She was boneless, melting. Tumbling. Her hips urged him on, racing into a heated climax that swallowed her. Dan felt her muscles tauten. He rocketed forward to a shattering climax, inflamed by the same inferno.

Rolling off her, he wrapped his arms around her. She rested her head in the crook of his shoulder.

He chuckled. "I think after that you can say we pleased each other."

Millie floated down to earth. Reaching up, she kissed his neck. She kissed his chest, too, and toyed with the springy mat of his hair. "And I can't print a word of it."

He tipped her chin up, kissing her full on the mouth. "I give you permission to print the whole thing."

She caught more of his playful spirit. He was making what could have been a difficult situation easy for her. "All right." She started to get up.

"Where do you think you're going?" His hands remained firmly on her waist, preventing her from leaving. Impulsively, he kissed the base of her spine, then licked the spot with his tongue.

She gasped. "To get my pad and pencil." He hauled her back and she fell flat on top of him. He wrapped his arms and legs around her. "What are you doing, Dan?"

His hand skittered up and down her body. "Frisking you. I must say I've never frisked a woman this way before. Put that in your book, too."

She giggled. He found her ticklish spots. "No fair." She rocked on top of him, finding any part of his flesh she could, giving him back the same treatment. Playing, and not sleeping after sex was a new experience for her. Everything with Dan seemed new.

He rolled over and pinned her beneath him. "I claim my prize."

"It's not over until the fat lady sings," she said, nipping his neck.

"Oh, yeah?" In a flash her arms were above her head, her wrists clamped in one hand. He stared down at her with stormy eyes. "Now, let me show you what it's like to mess around with the law." He knew her body, knew what made her writhe beneath him. He used this knowledge to his advantage.

"Oh, no. . . ." She moaned. "You're not fair."

He showed no mercy. "It's a tough world, lady."

She arched toward him. "Very—tough," she agreed, kissing him.

As quickly as it started, the play erupted into passion. This time he took her swiftly, masterfully. She loved it, matching his thrusts with a wildness she didn't realize she was capable of. He took her up, suspending her on the edge, then buried his face in her breasts as they fell into the abyss of ecstasy.

"Bells. I hear bells," she murmured, smiling.

He heard bells, too, and silently swore. It wasn't bells. It was the phone.

He kissed her brow, then leaned his forehead against hers, waiting for his breathing to return to normal.

"I'm sorry, Millie. I have to answer it." He liberally hurled oaths at the invention even as he lifted the receiver. "Yes," he snapped.

The jumble of words in his ear was almost incoherent—and reminiscent of another time. Wasach had put a curse on him.

"Stay calm. This isn't your first. Did you call the ambulance? Good. They'll probably get there before I do. Just hang on. I'm on my way." As he hung up, Millie hurriedly handed him his shirt.

"What happened?" she cried frantically as she struggled into her own clothing. "What's wrong?"

Dan zipped up his pants, swearing. "The baby's coming more than a week early." She finished dressing and he grabbed her hand, propelling her out the door.

"What baby?" she asked.

"We're about to become parents, Millie."

Baby? Parents? "Whoa there, Murdock. Have I missed something here, or are you a faster worker than I thought?"

"Millie." He tugged her toward the car. "I'm the slowest worker in the world, couldn't you tell? This is one man who's going to need a lot of rehearsing."

In a pig's eye, she thought. "I'll take notes."

He laughed and got her into her seat. "Like hell you will. Buckle up."

"What about my book?"

"Forget it. We'll write our own."

But she couldn't forget it. Or the life she led, which had nothing to do with chasing crooks, outfoxing an extortionist, umpiring a team of ex-cons, or racing through the midnight streets to deliver some premature baby.

She could only wonder what other surprises Dan had in store for her.

Eight

Dan told her about Rosita and the possibility that her second might be born at home, too. He boasted proudly about his namesake. They discussed almost everything they could think of—save the most important topic.

Each other.

It was as if the phone call had broken the tenuous link they'd forged. Dan's frustration took many forms. He wanted to tell her why he'd been dancing around most of the questions she had asked. It wasn't like him to be indirect, especially since by being with her, he agreed implicitly to talk with her. He was pretty sure Millie would do her homework. If it were up to him, he'd tell her about his Uncle Jack, the stain on the family name, everything. But it wasn't up to him.

Aware that her interest in him stemmed from a business arrangement, his needs surprised him.

But for Lana, he'd lived alone all of his adult life. He'd had his share of women—nice ones and demanding ones, pretty ones and not-so-pretty ones. A long-term relationship to him meant a series of stages one went through. After Lana, marriage hadn't been important. The years had drifted by, piling one on top of the other.

Aimlessly.

With Millie it had been different from the first, he realized with a shock. He'd never thought of her as a date or as someone to fill a vacancy in one of his temporary relationships. By reason of avoidance of the "love" word, they seemed to have elevated Topic A to an extreme significance, putting off the inevitable for a better time.

Millie was also experiencing a surge of another emotion. Guilt. She'd forgotten everything when Dan was making love with her. She'd let her body be played like a violin by a virtuoso. And she'd begun to realize that she could still feel, could still yearn to be loved by a caring man.

Sighing, she closed her eyes and tried to conjure up her husband's face. She'd deeply loved him—but now couldn't get a clear picture of him. From the years of advice she'd given to widows in her Ask Ms. M. column, she knew letting go of the guilt was part of the process of acceptance after a spouse dies.

How often had she responded to the anguish and guilt in letters by surviving spouses? Let it go, live your life, you have a right to find your happiness. She'd written it all, believed it when she wrote it for millions of readers.

Now all she had to do was convince herself.

With its red light flashing, Dan's car sped through the streets. He hoped the ambulance had arrived and that there'd be no need for his services. "Have you ever witnessed the birth of a baby?" he asked Millie.

Did he think she lived in the dark ages? she thought. She'd seen countless women sweat, grimace, scream, clutch, push, groan, and scream at their husbands—on television. In the movies. On stage.

"Are you kidding?" she boasted, glad to have the conversation directed to a neutral topic. "Lots of times."

He let out a long whistle, then took a curve well past the speed limit. "Rosy will be glad to see you. As a woman, you can probably appreciate that. You can help me then, if the ambulance hasn't arrived."

Millie sat up with a start. Her stomach did a queasy nosedive. She admitted the truth about her so-called television "crash course" in birthing. "Especially on late-night reruns of *Ben Casey*. I'd only get in your way."

Dan shook his head. Millie bit her lip. She folded and unfolded her hands, as if trying to keep them warm. He squeezed her leg. "Don't freeze up on me now, honey. Giving birth is the most beautiful act in the world.

"Tell you what. We'll make believe this is a television show. Rosy's the star, you're the supporting cast. I'm the director. I'll coach you through it."

The image was too real. Maybe Dan and her brother didn't think anything about delivering babies, but it wasn't her game. What happened if the baby was a breech? She prayed the paramedics had already whisked the laboring mother to the hospital. Failing that, she fervently prayed, let the mother-to-be order her out of the bedroom.

Millie tossed her hair back with shaky fingers. She managed a wobbly smile, ashamed of herself. "Does this sort of thing happen often?"

He laughed. "Lord, no. This is only my second delivery."

"And here I thought all you did was apprehend hoods and thugs. You're going to make a terrific midwife."

He pulled around a car, then gunned the motor. "No, I'm not. And yes, most of the time I do arrest criminals, or push paper, or give testimony at trials."

"And then the Pied Piper rehabilitates them," she said, patting his arm.

He sailed through a red light. "Better than arresting, booking, and prosecuting them all over again. Costs society too much."

"Bull, Murdock," she replied, again in possession of her intellect. "You do it because you're an old softie."

"Bull, Millie. I do it because cops are trained to protect society. Don't you dare ruin my Humphrey Bogart image. Keep this out of your book."

She practically leaped off the seat. "Enough. I've got my agent breathing down my neck on one side and you breathing down the other side. I've long since spent the advance money, and so far you've given me nothing. The deal was that you agreed to see the chapter. Before you know it, though, I'll be going home . . ."

He felt a tight ache in his throat. Their love-making meant more to him than to her. "What are you talking about?"

She heard the despair in his voice. "I live in New Jersey. My family is there. My life is there. You knew I was renting."

He struggled to keep quiet, then exploded. "Millie, your timing stinks!"

She made an effort to joke with him, to ignore the censure in his tone. "Oh, for goodness' sakes, what are we arguing about? Here we are about to become parents."

Privately, she agreed with him. Her timing did stink. So did the woman's whose baby decided it needed Dan to repeat his Dr. Casey routine.

The Lopez house, a two-storied white clapboard, was located in a middle-class neighborhood, not far from the beach. A fanning breeze riffled through her hair as Millie closed her car door and glanced around. The homes were situated on neatly tended plots. Instead of grass, many of the lawns were painted green rock, landscaped with islands of cactus varieties.

"Too much sand around here," Dan said. "Besides, it saves mowing."

He ran up the steps and rang the bell. It was immediately opened by his young namesake. Young

Daniel was a handsome, stockily built boy with luminous hazel-brown eyes, layers of midnight-black hair, and two adorable dimples.

"The ambulance isn't here yet," Daniel said. He grabbed Dan's hand, pulling him inside the cool hallway. "Mom's gonna have the baby at home, I think. She went to Lamaze classes, but Dad couldn't make it all the time, and I think he's scared. She should have taken me instead." His reedy voice quavered.

Dan ruffled the boy's hair. "You did fine, Daniel. Wait here, Millie."

Her relief was short-lived. Daniel touched her hand, beseeching her with pleading eyes.

"My mama may need you. Dad's nervous. Please help her." His tears were near the surface.

Millie smiled weakly, gathered her resolve, and nodded. This wasn't like any television script she'd ever seen. But who could deny a child with such beguiling eyes? He'd break women's hearts in years to come.

At the bedroom door, Millie hesitated. Rosita's husband, Manuel, wasn't nearly as calm as his son. In his mid-thirties, Manuel was a handsome adult version of young Daniel. He was also sweating as profusely as the pregnant woman on the bed.

Rosita tried to smile when she saw Dan, but was quickly gripped by pain. He introduced Millie, then timed a strong contraction, then another. Ambulance or not, he thought, this baby was going to be making a neighborhood appearance pretty soon.

He gave Millie a crash course in coaching. Petrified that she might make a mistake, she followed his orders to the letter, coaching Rosita as though both their lives as well as the unborn baby's depended on it. Dan ordered Manuel to bring clean towels and a basin of boiled water.

Manuel fled the room gladly, his eyes close to hysterical. Dan wiped Rosita's face with a damp cloth. "Next time, young lady, you're going to the hospital a month early, if I have to take you there myself."

He glanced at Millie. "You're doing fine, coach. When your time comes, it'll be a piece of cake."

She barely had time to let Dan's words register. He'd intimated that one day she'd be repeating Rosita's experience.

Millie knew if she lived to be a hundred, she'd never forget Dan bringing Rosita's baby girl into the world, or the look of sheer pleasure on everyone's face when the infant let out its first lusty cry, bringing the rest of the family on the run.

Tears streamed down Rosita's face. "Oh, thank you, Dan. You've helped me give birth to the baby daughter I've always wanted."

Dan winked at Millie. Her knees were buckling, her mouth was dry as dust, but her spirits soared. She'd been part of the most wonderful miracle. And she hadn't fainted.

"Piece of cake," Dan said, grinning. "Right, coach?"

She nodded. Her throat was too full to speak.

The paramedics rushed into the room just as Dan was swabbing out the baby's nose and mouth to clear the passageways. He swaddled the infant in a clean towel and laid her on Rosita's stomach. "Rosy, you did great. She's all yours, guys."

"Thanks, Murdock. We owe you a great favor for our precious *hija*."

They waited in the living room while a paramedic cut the umbilical cord and helped with the placenta. Later, Rosita asked for Millie, who helped her put on a fresh nightgown.

She stroked Millie's arm. "What is your full name?"

"Millicent Dolores Gordon."

Rosita and Manuel beamed. "We will never forget you, Millie," Rosita said. She lifted the tiny bundle. "Meet Millicent Dolores Lopez. Would you like to be the first to hold her?"

Millie bawled all the way home—big, fat, sloppy tears. Each time she tried to stop, a fresh flood of tears trickled down her cheeks. "Do you realize," she asked, sniffling into a tissue, "we each have a child named after us?"

Dan smiled at her. Her nose was shiny red. Her dark hair was a tangled nest around her face. But her blue eyes gleamed with pride. He thought she'd never looked more beautiful. Millie was lost in the euphoria of what she'd lived through.

"As soon as I'm in New York," she bubbled, "I'm going to empty out FAO Schwarz. Nothing is too good for my namesake. Of course, I'll get an equal number of toys for your little Daniel. Can't have him getting jealous."

Dan's brow furrowed. Was she pushing him to say don't go? "So you're really going back?"

She hesitated. "Eventually. I only came here for a change of scenery."

He stared stonily ahead. "I'm usually a workaholic," she added, sort of as a verbal footnote. "My work's been sliding lately."

He understood her feelings, perhaps more than she did herself. She'd come to Florida to close a chapter in her life. Was she telling him she was eager to be back among the family and friends she'd known all her life? Or was she waiting for him to say the words that would keep her here?

The sun, a fiery orange and red ball, dipped below the horizon. One minute it was day; the next, a soft, soothing night with a vast throw of twinkling stars above them as Dan walked Millie to her door. He kissed her and left. They were both bushed. He wasn't in the mood for small talk—not when he needed his wits about him to plan. . . .

Millie lounged on the patio, still floating on a cloud. She'd slept well, alternately dreaming of Dan and her infant namesake. She wrapped the phone cord around her fingers.

"Let me get this straight," Wylie said. "Yesterday you and Dan became parents. And here I was worried about you. What do they put in the food down there? Fertility pills?"

Millie giggled silently. If Wylie only knew! "Not real parents, goose. Rosy named their first son for Dan seven years ago. This baby is named for me. I have a vested interest in little Millie."

She told the story in fits and starts, downplaying her part in the process, extolling Dan's coolness and emergency medical prowess, and praising Rosita's courage.

"I'm beginning the chapter today," Millie announced euphorically. "Dan's an unsung hero."

"You mean it's still not written?" Wylie pounced on the admission. "Hang up and get to work, dammit. I've run out of usable excuses. If you can't work there, come home. Do I have to remind you there's a law against spending unearned money—unless you want to hock your house and give it back?"

Nothing Wylie said dampened Millie's spirits. She waltzed into her temporary office and turned on the computer. She'd never missed a deadline yet.

Daniel J. Murdock's favorite phrase is, "piece of cake." This intriguing detective sergeant resembles a silver-tipped Cary Grant, is as closemouthed about his private life as Gary Cooper, and protects his tough-guy Humphrey Bogart image. He is not your run-of-the-mill detective, believe me. I speak from firsthand experience. In the short time I've known the man, he's placed himself in the line of danger to save my life; introduced me to a group of softball-playing reformed ex-convicts proudly bearing the "team colors"—Murdock's Maniacs— on their caps; and coached me as I helped this multitalented man deliver a baby.

And I think I might be in love with him.

Sighing, she stood up, spreading her fingers across the small of her back. She flipped through her Rolodex, found the number she needed, and dialed. Chip Harvey was a computer whiz, a first-rate researcher, and her friend. She quickly explained the book's concept and what she needed.

"I take it you need this stuff yesterday," Chip quizzed shrewdly.

She chuckled, pleased she'd called him. "Or the day before. It's deadline time. You know how hairy that can be."

"Not to worry, Millie, darlin'. As we say in the trade—piece of cake."

Now where had she heard that before? Millie smiled at the reference.

Dan slumped into the chair in front of Wasach's desk and tried to look exhausted. He crossed his long legs at the ankle and stretched his arms above his head. He yawned, then yawned again. Thank heaven for reflex actions when you needed them.

Wasach narrowed his eyes. "You want a vacation? What for?"

Dan fixed his eyes on a spot above the chief's shoulder. He was being deliberately vague. "Three days. I've got the time off coming. Call it a paternity leave."

Wasach sat back, skeptical. "Everything all right with your folks? Your dad isn't upset about your being included in this Gordon's book, is he?"

"He and my mother are overseas. They'll be back soon. Anyway, I've decided to wait and see what Millie writes."

Wasach nodded. "What about her? You know how important this is for us. How are you going to explain to her she's got to take a few days' break in her schedule?"

"Don't worry," Dan assured him. "You'll get your story. I have an idea she can use the time off. She looked pretty pooped to me yesterday. Besides being in the stakeout, she helped deliver Rosy Lopez's baby. She told me she needs to work on her Ask Ms. M. column."

"All right," Wasach said. "Three days. Then I want you back here. Louie's case is coming to trial." He tossed a pink-banded cigar across the desk. "Here, Detective Sergeant Daddy. The guys and I pitched in. Congratulations."

Dan's brows lifted. "You're all heart, Wasach. How about one for Rosy's husband?"

Wasach sat back. "Give him yours. We're on a tight budget."

Dan caught the innuendo. Whenever the chief had something to say, he never missed a trick in selling his case. Now he was saying, Take your three days, Murdock, but never forget we're depending on you.

Dan let the insinuation roll off his back. He had something more important to think about. Millie. He knew the perfect inducement to get her away from the computer. But first, he needed to stop at a toy store. . . .

•   •   •

Dan took Millie to the hospital to visit Rosita and her new daughter. As they left, Millie couldn't stop talking about the infant. She'd had little experience with babies and had been awed by the tiny girl's perfection. She stopped in mid-sentence, though, when she caught Dan grinning at her.

"What are you smirking about?" she asked.

He pulled her to him and kissed the tip of her nose. "I was thinking how lucky we are that Rosy didn't have twins."

Millie's brows arched. "I'll have you know that I'm a twin."

"In that case, I take it back," he said good-naturedly. "Do you and your twin look much alike?"

"No. My brother Kipp is tall." She held her hand above her head. "Six-foot three. He's broad-shoul-dered." She winked. "He's the one who shaves."

"Sounds identical to me," he teased. "Are you two close?"

She nodded. "Very. I'll be glad to see him again. I miss him."

She didn't notice the shadow that crossed Dan's face, nor was she paying much attention when he commented, "There're always airplanes if you lived here."

"What now?" she asked, rummaging in her purse for her sunglasses as they walked out into the bright sunlight.

"Now," he said offhandedly, "we go bear hunting."

"Bear hunting!" She halted in mid step, intrigued.

He took her elbow. "Close your mouth, Millie. I'm offering you the chance of a lifetime. Think of the publicity for your book, if we were to catch a bear. You can put the picture on the cover."

Millie didn't know if it was fate or coincidence. All she knew was that being with Dan was exhilarating but, at the rate she was going, her publisher would definitely demand repayment.

"Bears in Florida?" She still didn't trust him.

He *tsked*. "Ever hear of Gentle Ben?"

Who hadn't? In her best lead-on-MacDuff voice, she said, "Bear hunting it is."

Her only question was whether they had to go to Alaska to snare one. She ignored the scolding sound of Wylie's voice in her mind, demanding that she get cracking.

Dan congratulated himself. He'd passed the first hurdle. Now for the second. "Pack an overnight case, Millie. Oh, and you might want to bring along a dress for the evening—in case the bear is hiding out in a fancy restaurant."

Her antennae flashed on, along with her jolting nerves. This had nothing to do with official business or he would have told her. She was making a decision with irrevocable implications. "Is this bear likely to need a bathing suit, too?"

"Don't be silly." He broke into a spontaneous grin. "Bears swim in the nude."

Was it her imagination, or did he linger on that last word?

"Aim."

Millie aimed, sighting down the barrel with a demonic squint.

"Pull."

She pulled. "I can't stand it!" she fumed. "The stupid can is still standing. They all are."

"My fault," Dan said cheerfully. "I should have said squeeze."

She made a moue. "It won't help. You can recite the alphabet backward and I'd still miss the dumb can."

She'd been at it for half an hour. Every empty soda can stood up straight and tall on the fence posts. They were in a clearing in the middle of a field. Flanking it were stands of tulip oak trees draped with Spanish moss. Nearby a meandering stream gurgled past a stone waterfall on its way to the Gulf.

They had passed Weeki Wachi on Highway 19 when Dan slowed the car, halting on the shoulder. "Why are we stopping here?" she'd asked.

He had pointed to a sign. "I thought you might like to read that."

She'd gasped in amazement. "I thought you were kidding. There really is a sign warning about bears."

Dan had looked pleased with himself. "Detectives never lie. Put that in the book. We have brown bears in Florida. I bet you thought all we had were alligators."

As they drove on, he had regaled her with bear stories, each more preposterous than the last. When he'd bragged about people flying in from Alaska to check out whether the Florida bears were really larger, she'd finally scoffed. "You're lying."

He'd winked. "But of course. It's a great tourist attraction."

Tourist attraction or not, she still couldn't hit the side of a barn. If she did see a bear, she'd run for cover. Her shoulders slumped. "Dan, we might as well quit. I'm a total failure."

He wasn't about to. Not with the surprise he planned. "You need a pith helmet."

Was he mad?

"What for?"

"In case you bag a tiger instead, silly. Wait here."

He went to the car, popped open the trunk, and scooted back with a large bag. With a great flourish, he pulled out a pith helmet. He plunked it on her head before she knew what was happening.

Oversized, it fell over her eyes and nose. She couldn't see a thing. "Very funny," she muttered. "Now I've got a toilet bowl on my head."

"Pith helmet," he corrected her. He tapped the helmet, listening to the hollow sound. "Perfect fit. I wish I had a camera."

The helmet bobbed up and down. She gestured broadly with her hands. "I can't hit a blade of grass," she said, "let alone a bear or a tiger."

"Don't be silly," he said. He was having the time of his life. "I'll coach you through it."

She groaned. "Where have I heard that before? I'm getting tired. Who can shoot playing blind-man's buff?"

"Patience, Millie. One last time."

"What are you doing?"

She felt his chest against her back as his hands covered hers. The scent of his cologne surrounded her. Even if she wanted to, she couldn't think straight, let alone shoot straight.

He extended her arms then tipped the pistol skyward. "Shhh, there's a bear up in that tree. Now I want you to draw gently on the trigger. Squeeze and pull!"

The report of the bullet broke the stillness. Millie jerked backward. Dan steadied her. He plucked off her helmet, twirling her around. There was a big, wide grin on his face. "You did it!" He hugged her. "You bagged your bear!"

In spite of herself, the child in her wanted to believe. Dan made it sound so possible. "I don't see a thing," she said, looking around and feeling foolish.

"Ye of little faith." He scooped up the bag, grabbed her hand, and darted over to a tree. "What do you see?"

"See?" She kicked at a clump of leaves. "Spanish moss. It's on all the trees. . . . Shouldn't we be going?" she asked dejectedly.

He picked up the dark, round ball of moss. With one hand he held the clump over her head and drew her to him with the other. His eyes glowed. "Happy New Year, Millie," he said softly. "That wasn't moss you shot. That was magic mistletoe. It grows in these tulip oaks. For a kiss, the mistletoe turns into a bear."

It was wonderful to play his game. She steeped herself in his presence, his scent, the deepness of his voice. She wanted to kiss him, to make love with him.

"What do you say, Millie?" His voice was now

quietly serious. His eyes held her mesmerized. "Shall we see if there's magic left in the world?"

He stroked her cheek. She didn't want to think about complex issues, or of going home, or the reasons behind Dan's reticence each time she questioned him about his family.

If he wanted magic, she wanted it, too. She wrapped her arms around his neck, lifting her face to his. When his lips touched hers she let herself believe in magic. Transported beyond mere earth, she let herself feel the magic.

Excitement built quickly. Dan had promised her magic, but found himself enraptured instead. Millie's body, her pliant flesh melding with his, set him on fire. He wanted to stay there with her forever in their private world.

When had the air smelled so pure, the rustling of the trees been so lyrical, the trill of a bird so sweet, or the sky above so blue? He was conscious of everything, yet mostly he was aware of the woman in his arms. And yet he had never been so wary of the fact that her book stood between them.

When the kiss ended, they smiled into each other's eyes, willing to submerge their doubts for a little while longer. Dan eased away from her and surreptitiously reached into the bag. "Voilà, your magic bear!"

Millie's throat clogged as she reached for the stuffed animal. Dan had gone to great lengths to give her the teddy and she was touched. "I love her. Thank you."

Dan beamed, although he would have preferred to hear her say, I love you.

"You're welcome."

He had scoured the toy shops to find the perfect pink teddy bear. It had round, soulful black eyes, a button nose, and a sweet smile. A shiny red heart dotted with tiny rhinestones adorned its chest, and on its pink, ruffled skirt were the words *Love Me*. He hoped she'd get the message.

"Now you can forget all those other times when you went home empty-handed from the board-walk in Wildwood, New Jersey."

A tear rolled down her cheek. "Oh, Dan. She's beautiful. She's my Bernadette." She flung herself into his arms, laughing and kissing him.

"You really are a magician," she said. She gave him a brilliant smile, wishing she had some magic dust herself. She would cast a spell on him to erase the pain of his uncle's death. Chip Harvey had called back. The Murdock name had been dragged through a media circus in New York City some years ago. Detective Jack Murdock had been killed by the mob, then revealed to be a cop on the take.

Dan clasped her tightly to him. He was caught between loyalty to his father and wondering whether the fickle public would remember or care about his uncle. "I wish I were a magician, Millie," he told her silently. "I really do. . . ."

Nine

Dan patted the bear seated in the pith helmet on Millie's knee. She steadfastly refused to be parted from either. They were traveling the last five miles of their trip. He couldn't remember spending a better day.

Neither could Millie. She loved listening to his voice as he pointed out places of interest. She drank in the sight of him, his broad shoulders and chest, his strong arms, the easy manner in which he drove. He was completely relaxed and so sure of himself, she envied him.

"Why Bernadette?" he asked, watching her fondle the bear's pink ears.

She felt a familiar tightness gather in her stomach. Choosing a baby's name was an exercise in futility she'd indulged in a long time ago. "If we'd had a child we'd have named it either Bernadette or Bernard. It means brave as a bear or courageous. You have to be courageous to get through life. They're strong names, good names to live by." She couldn't hide the wistfulness that crept into her voice.

"Why didn't you adopt?" Dan asked. He knew she wanted children. He'd seen the yearning and hunger in her eyes when she held Rosita's baby. She was wealthy in her own right; her husband had been a corporate attorney. It hadn't been money.

Millie gnawed her bottom lip. It was a while before she spoke. "It never came up."

He was moved by the simple declaration, more so since he didn't believe a word of it. He suddenly realized the truth. "Your husband didn't want to adopt a child, is that it?" There was a thread of censure in his tone.

Tears, unbidden and unwanted, singed her eyes. Frank had said he wanted children—his own. She'd come to realize that deep in his psyche his inability to have children was tied up with fears and doubts about his manhood. "Does it matter?" she murmured.

Dan watched her with compassion, his expression gentling. In the late afternoon, the sun streamed through the window, sending shafts of light through her hair. He stared straight ahead again. "I was just wondering where I'd be if my parents hadn't adopted me."

Millie was caught off guard, too stunned to speak for a moment. "You're adopted?"

He shrugged. "Yes. So's my sister. We came as a pair. The Murdocks didn't have the heart to break us up, thank God. I was four years old, not exactly the age when most people want to adopt. Too bad your husband never met my folks."

The more she learned of this complex man, the more she realized how easy it would be to love him. He spoke so naturally, so lovingly, about his adoptive parents. "What happened to your natural parents?" she asked.

He hesitated. His eyes reflected remembered pain. "Dad was a chemist. One night he and my mother went to the small plant he owned. They were on their way to a party, dressed in their evening things. I remember that my mother looked lovely in her yellow gown. Dad had a special government order he wanted to check on. Somehow two vials of chemicals must have been knocked off a shelf. The chemicals merged and exploded. They died instantly."

She squeezed his hand. She could imagine the horrible scene. "Oh, Dan, I'm so sorry. Weren't there other members of your family who could raise you and your sister?" How cruel to compound one tragedy on top of another, tearing innocent children away from their relatives.

A muscle worked in his jaw and a fierce expression clouded his face. When he spoke, his voice was stoic with disillusionment and grief. "I don't know the details, but no. There was no one able to take the two of us."

Knowing the accomplished, caring man Dan had become, her heart swelled with pride. She understood at last the reason behind his passionate protection of his adoptive family. "May I use this in the book?"

"Sure, why not? I'm proud of being a Murdock."

Then tell me the rest of it, she begged silently. *Trust me not to hurt your folks.* She tried to break down the last barrier separating them.

"You know, Dan," she began cautiously, "other than the history of your marriage, that's the most you've said about your past. You have this habit of answering a question with a question. Why?"

He sidestepped the issue, joking. "Maybe I'm a psychiatrist in hiding.

"I'll tell you one thing," he added, getting back to the subject uppermost in his mind. "If you were my wife, we'd have children, one way or the other." His mouth curved up, lightening the mood in the car. "Not that I wouldn't try my best to have them the old-fashioned way, you understand."

Her nails dug into her palms. She didn't want to think about how it really had been with Frank. She'd begged to adopt a child until she was blue in the face. For a while she had thought he was refusing because of her busy career. She had promised to put it on hold to raise a family. Even Kipp, who normally didn't interfere, had once broached the subject with Frank, assuring him he'd love an adopted baby. Frank had thrown every argument back in their faces. He wouldn't budge. If it wasn't his biological child, he didn't want the headache.

Frank had been a wonderful man in every other respect, and she had loved him, yet clearly part of her still resented his resolute stand. She had nothing to show for all those years of marriage. It would have been different if it had been her choice, too. Plenty of women chose to be childless. Child-free, they called it now. She wasn't one of them.

"Stop it," she said abruptly, feeling disloyal. "You don't know how it was."

Dan frowned. "I can guess," he said, then wanted to kick himself for his *faux pas*. It was like a sore tooth. He was jealous of a dead man he'd never met, who couldn't defend himself. Wonderful, he thought, disgusted with himself. And that, he supposed, was a new definition of love. After thinking it would never happen to him, he had fallen for Millie like a ton of bricks. He was making a first-class botch of it. He considered telling her, then realized the timing was wrong.

"Sorry," he said. "That was none of my business."

"What are your plans?" she asked, directing the conversation away from herself. "Are you hoping to make chief someday? Readers will want to know."

The answer came swiftly. "I have no ambition to play the budget game with a mayor and city council." He wanted to demand that she tell him about her husband. He didn't give a damn about the book or readers. He wanted to crawl inside her head. "Millie, I know I haven't exactly answered everything you've asked me, but there's a reason."

"What's the reason?" She held her breath, willing him to trust her.

"Give me until next week. One way or the other, you'll have your answer to my less-than-candid behavior."

She dared to hope. "A week, no more. I'm working on a deadline. If I can't get one good chapter, I'll scrap it and resurrect some material I wrote a while ago. My publisher wants results, not excuses."

So does Wasach, he thought. "Fair enough."

They had made a little progress, she mused. She'd settle for that. "What's happening with Louie?"

"His trial won't come up for a while."

Dan slowed the car, turning off the main highway onto a side road. A sign directed them to the Ocean Resort.

Dan chuckled. "But when it does, we've got a little surprise for Louie. Spike Harvey resents being in jail while Louie's breathing the nice outside air with his friends. Naturally, Ben and I have been making regular visits to Spike, seeding his anger. He's decided to cooperate in exchange for immunity. We're keeping him under protective custody until the trial."

Millie stopped playing with Bernadette's ear. This was good news. "But I thought Spike was still in jail."

Dan smiled crookedly. "Can you think of a better place than a jail cell to keep someone in protective custody?"

She punched his arm with the bear, laughing. She looked at him with admiration. "You conniving devil! Spike's in jail one way or the other, and you get Louie, too. With your little scheme you don't have to pay police personnel to work extra duty. That's good, Murdock."

"Yeah," he drawled, delighted to see her in a better frame of mind.

"Is Louie really dangerous or just mouthy?"

"He's unpredictable. The company he keeps makes him dangerous. Now what do you say we skip all this work talk and enjoy ourselves? Here we are."

Here was the Ocean Resort, a sprawling complex on lush grounds. They drove alone a palm-lined road leading to the main building, which looked out over the ocean. There were tennis courts, three Olympic-sized swimming pools, outdoor snack bars, and a complete gym. For the swimmers and sailors the resort offered snorkeling and sailing, and for the fishermen, rental boats.

"Wait until you taste the food," Dan said. "Culinary masterpieces." He parked the car near the manager's office. "Chef Henri's from France. He fell in love with an American exchange student, followed her here, and made all her parents' favorite dishes. That's what I call strategy. He doesn't work in the kitchen anymore. He prefers meeting the people, but the standards are the same. He rules with an iron skillet."

Millie carried her overnight bag and Bernadette, falling into step beside Dan. Adult or not, she'd been away from the dating scene a long time, and she'd never checked into a hotel with a man who wasn't her husband.

"Do you come here often?" she asked. Lord, she couldn't believe she'd asked such a dumb thing. Dan was a grown man, and she could attest to his sexual appetite.

He gave her a quizzical look. "I plan to." Dry amusement rumbled in his voice.

Jealousy stabbed her, but she managed to keep her voice light. "I can see why." Needing a moment, she paused to admire the vivid tropical flowers.

His lips twitched. "It's a very romantic setting, don't you agree?"

"Very." She smiled until it hurt, remembering her advice to her readers. *Whatever you do, ladies, don't show a man you're jealous.* She wasn't aware she was clutching Bernadette by the throat.

"You're killing your bear," he remarked casually, then turned to hide his smirk of satisfaction.

Embarrassed at being so easily read, Millie immediately relaxed her death grip on the bear's neck. Ms. M. would handle the situation brilliantly, she thought, but plain Millicent Dolores Gordon put her foot in her mouth. So much for sophistication.

Dan turned back to her. He put down the suitcase and placed his hands on her shoulders. "My parents love it here. They've been telling me about this place for the past two years." He rubbed his knuckles over her cheek, looking deeply into her eyes. "Millie," he said softly, "I've never been here before. Never had a reason to come before."

Immense relief washed over her. "Thank you for that, Dan." She grinned. "I'm famished."

"Me, too. I phoned for reservations. We can change in our room, then have dinner."

That answered her next question. He expected her to share his room. "Aren't you taking a lot for granted?"

His gray eyes were unreadable. "Am I?"

Who was she kidding? She wasn't a coy adolescent. She knew exactly what his invitation had meant. She'd made love with him and couldn't get it out of her mind. "One room will be fine."

He leaned over to kiss her gently. "You won't be sorry, Millie. I may not write an advice column, but I do understand. Each step you're taking now is a new one. It is for me, too. And," he added, stroking her cheek, "if it helps you, I'm a little nervous, too."

They were given the honeymoon suite. Millie never learned if Dan had arranged it or if the hotel really was full. They had a sweeping panoramic view of the ocean. Sliding glass doors led to a secluded terrace and deck area with a private heart-shaped hot tub. Purple, pink, and white geraniums lined the walls, along with potted palms, cactus, and bougainvillea.

The opulent suite consisted of a large living room that flowed into an enormous bedroom decorated in muted earth tones. A compact kitchen and a bathroom with a sunken tub and indoor sauna completed the suite. But it was the mirrors above the bed that held Millie's attention.

"Dan," she said weakly, wishing she were a trim twenty-year-old. She set the bear and her bag down. "I'm over thirty."

He put his arms around her. "So am I. You promise not to look at the ceiling?" He carefully refrained from giving her the same promise. There wasn't a spot on Millie's body he hadn't seen and kissed, and wanted to kiss again—soon. He silently applauded the decorator.

She sat down on the bed, shaking her head.

He sat down next to her. "What?" He took his gun from his ankle holster and laid it on the night table.

"I was just thinking, if my readers could see me now, they'd say—"

"That I was a very lucky man." He took her hand, massaged the palm with his thumb, then kissed her lips.

Millie's heart began to hammer, and she wrapped her arms around him. She wanted to remember everything about him.

"They've decorated this suite beautifully," she said.

"It's the French influence. You must be starved. It isn't every day you shoot a pink bear. Let's change, or we'll never get out of here."

Wanting to look glamorous for Dan, she had brought along a strapless red silk dress, high-heeled sling-back pumps, and dark patterned stockings. Knowing his preference for long hair, she left hers down, brushing it until it shone. The light caught highlights of shimmering amber. She wore a rhinestone comb tucked behind one ear.

She took special care with her makeup, applying smoky blue eye shadow and dark mascara to emphasize her eyes. She dotted lip gloss over her pale red lipstick. The look on Dan's face told her she hadn't wasted her efforts. She smiled, fluttering her lashes, then giggled. Her femme fatale imitation was ruined.

He slipped his arms around her waist and nuzzled her neck. "You're making it hard to leave this room. Mmm, you smell good, too."

"Dan . . . I thought you said you were hungry." He was nibbling her ear and she couldn't think straight. He kissed her throat, then lowered his head to her breast.

"I am. I'm starved." He lightly kissed one nipple. "Well, these were made to feed a man's senses."

The muscles in her stomach coiled, and she pressed a hand to the back of his head. "Reservations," she mumbled.

"Right." His sigh was ragged. He straightened up reluctantly. "A real man would rip off your clothes and drag you to bed."

She couldn't resist teasing him. "A real man of thirty-six needs his protein."

Pretending to be affronted, he moved close to her. There was a mischievous gleam in his eye. "Are you suggesting I'm getting old?" He backed her against the wall, pinning her arms to her sides, and branded her with a stormy kiss. His hips ground against hers. "That's not old," he said, letting her feel his rising desire. "And neither is this."

His hands held her in a vise. He opened his mouth on hers, kissing her relentlessly until he heard a moan deep in her throat. He released her suddenly, leaving her breathless. His eyes were dark, his voice hoarse. "On second thought, if we don't get out of here, I'm going to skip the meal and get down to dessert."

Millie needed another kind of nourishment. She'd found it once in his arms. Boldly, she pushed aside his jacket and ran her hands up his chest. Her fingers worked on his patterned silk tie, loosening the knot.

"Not a bad idea, Murdock. Of course, we're all dressed and we do have reservations." As if it were a feather boa, she slid the tie up on the back of his neck, teasingly drawing him close until their lips were a breath apart. She smiled dreamily. "Come here." He willingly did what she asked, letting her fit her mouth to his, taking what she wanted. The tie floated to the floor.

When she let him come up for air, his eyes were glowing with desire. His hands skimmed her rib cage. "I've always admired a woman who knew what she wanted. You don't mind if I return the favor, do you?"

She shivered with delicious sensations. He removed the rhinestone comb from behind her ear.

"Be my guest," she said. He was, tracing the shape of her ear with his tongue until her bones felt as if they'd melt.

"My turn." Her hands dropped to his waist, fumbling with the belt. She kissed his chin, then ran her lips lightly up his face to his mouth. Satisfied that she was driving him as crazy as he was making her, she threw her head back and fluttered her lashes.

"I imagine," she murmured huskily, "in a place like this, at the height of the season and all, they'd be miffed if we didn't show."

Neither moved to the phone. The belt followed the tie. She kissed the pulse beat at the base of his throat.

"You're racing, Murdock." For good measure she made him race a little faster by blowing tiny breaths in his ear. "I didn't hear your answer, detective."

He found his voice on a croak. "Think of the happy couple who will inherit our reservation."

His arms went around her and he tugged at the zipper to her dress. She leaned into him, making low throaty sounds. He chuckled, then began slowly to lower the zipper.

He kissed her shoulder, the curve of her neck, and paved a whispery course to her other side, giving it the same meticulous attention. He turned her around, following the line of the zipper with his lips.

"Murdock." His name shuddered out of her. Her dress slithered down her body. She stepped out of it and pushed her stockings off. She wore only a strapless bra and bikini panties.

"Oh, baby, do I want you," he said huskily, turning her in his arms.

Her fingers were busy with the buttons of his shirt. She spread the shirt fabric wide and kissed his chest. Then she pushed the shirt off his shoulders, and it fell to the floor. "You're sure you don't mind missing the meal?" she teased.

"From what I hear"—he nibbled his way along the top of her breasts—"there's eating and there's drinking. Personally, I'd rather drink. I have this terrible thirst." He released the clasp on her bra, and took her breast in his mouth.

At the first touch of his lips hot electricity shot through her, fanning her desire into a full conflagration.

Dan flicked his tongue in erotic circles around her nipples. She could feel the very air heat. Her trembling fingers worked feverishly at his pants zipper. In a moment they faced each other undressed, with no thought of shyness.

Dan sat down on the bed. She knelt behind him, her arms around his waist, and trailed kisses along his spine. "What?" she asked, as he chuckled.

"I just realized it doesn't much matter where we are—car, hallway, hotel room, field, my house—it's going to end the same way. We might as well stay naked."

"What about food?"

He turned to her. Her face was flushed, her eyes glowing.

"The heck with food." He pressed her down on the bed and leaned over her. "We'll grow skinny together. There's someplace else I'd rather be."

"And where is that?" she murmured.

His gaze traveled slowly from one end of her body to the other. He poised over her, lifting her hips. "In you. Giving to you. Like this . . ."

Millie giggled, turning her face into his shoulder. "The mirror on the ceiling was a waste."

"A lot you know," he said, shifting her on top of him. "Where do you think I got my inspiration?"

"You promised!"

He shook his head. "No, I didn't. You did." She collapsed on him, laughing. "Are you trying to tell me," he growled, his mouth hovering near hers, "that my lovemaking was a joke?"

They'd made love twice, wildly, passionately, arousing each other until they erupted in a volcanic climax. The sun had long since dipped below the horizon. Except for a small shaft of flickering moonlight streaming through the window, the room was dark.

"No," she said. "I'm trying to tell you I'm starving. Oh, no, you don't!" She pushed his roaming hand away. "I'm really starving, as in let's eat. You shower first. I'll see what can be done with my dress."

"Why don't we order room service?" he grumbled. He trailed his fingers up her thigh. "Then I can eat what I want and you can eat what you want. By the way, I dare you to put this in your book."

The book. She'd forgotten all about the damned book. Forgotten that that was what had brought them together. His hands were incredibly arousing. He made her body tremble. She willed herself to relax, to reason calmly.

Dan wasn't the marrying kind. His bachelor life-style suited him. She wasn't the type to settle for a long-term affair, or a gun on the night table when she went to bed. The sooner she returned home, the better. Vacation romances rarely amounted to anything. If she didn't believe it, Ms. M. did. Right now she'd trust Ms. M.'s judgment over Millie Gordon's.

Dan brushed the hair back from her forehead, kissed her lightly, then patted her fanny. He picked up the phone and called the restaurant. Winking at her, he somberly told the maitre d' that they had been unavoidably detained. "Something came up," he said, while she choked. Smiling, he hung up. "He said there was no problem. We have a later seating for thirty minutes from now. Get out of bed, lazybones."

It took Millie a moment to stiffen her jellied

legs. Within half an hour they'd showered and dressed and were strolling arm in arm into the restaurant.

The maitre d' asked them to wait at the door.

Chef Henri, a tall, middle-aged man with a neatly trimmed dark beard, piercing blue eyes, and a firm handshake, came to greet them. He bowed in a courtly gesture over Millie's hand, and introduced himself.

"Your dear parents speak so highly of you, Dan," he said as he seated them at a table overlooking the ocean. "For my friends the Murdocks, I shall, with your permission, order for you." Pleased by the gesture, Dan thanked him.

"To start, you shall have salade Henri, followed by gratinée, fillet of sole duxelle farcie, sauce beurre blanc, julienne of vegetables, rice pilaf, with a dessert of fresh fruit sabayon."

Henri snapped his fingers. Instantly a white-coated waiter stepped forward and handed him a linen-swathed bottle of wine. Henri poured a small amount into a glass and handed it to Dan for his tasting approval. Then he filled Millie's glass.

"To cleanse the palate," he said, "and with my compliments, de Ladquette Pouilly Fumé. *C'est l'amour*," he added, beaming. "*Toujours l'amour*."

Dan grinned as Chef Henri left. "What a character. I like him. Did you understand everything he said? I sure as heck didn't."

She smiled, not answering. She saw that several other women in the room were gazing at Dan with open admiration. She couldn't blame them. Dressed in a beautifully tailored double-breasted dark blue Italian suit, his white dress shirt emphasizing his deep tan, Dan looked both dashing and handsome. For tonight, he was hers, whether he understood French or not.

Dan decided restraint wasn't his strong suit. Millie wasn't helping, sitting opposite him, her lips swollen from his kisses, her face flushed from their lovemaking, her hair tumbling down her back. She was gazing at him as if he were the most interesting dinner companion in the world. But he was always more comfortable with action over words.

He debated acknowledging that he loved her, deciding finally against it. Weren't those her own words of advice that he'd read over and over through the years? The very words that prompted his silence now.

"True love needs time to mature," she'd written so often it was her trademark. Ms. M. was an old-fashioned advice giver. He tried to meld that with Millie, the gorgeous hoyden with the tumbling mass of black hair, who sent his senses into the stratosphere, and whose blue eyes he saw in his dreams. They were one and the same, writing about a society in a sexual shambles, cautioning people not to act out of haste.

If she needed time, he'd give it to her. Another week. No more, he decided. Love made him an impatient man. In the meantime he'd check with the dean of his law school. He had more important things to do with his nights than sit in unmarked cars waiting to pounce on palookas and hoods.

He'd woo her, then ask her to marry him. If she said no, he'd lock her up in protective custody until she said yes. Of course, protective custody would be his house. First he'd have to come clean with the goods about his uncle. If he didn't, she'd rightfully wonder why he didn't trust her—writer or not.

Pleased with his decision, he dug into his food with gusto. "Great meal."

"Delicious," Millie said. Obviously, he hadn't noticed she was merely poking at her food. She'd been replaying what he'd said in the car: "If you were my wife, we'd have children one way or the other."

She flushed, remembering his next line. "Not that I wouldn't try my best to have babies the old-fashioned way." And his best was very good indeed.

Hours later, Millie again recalled Dan's words. She had assumed she knew all about sex. If she'd felt excitement with Dan before, it was nothing to the way he made love with her now. It was as if he'd passed a turning point in his life. He took her by storm, sheathing himself in her with turbulent ungovernable passion.

The scent of him was rich, compellingly masculine. His body was hard and firm. His fingers found the center of her femininity, trapping her in his power until she could tolerate being held off no longer. "Dan, please," she implored him, digging her nails into his back.

That was what he wanted to hear. She needed his essence. Increasing the tempo, he exploded with her.

Millie drew the sheet up over her body. Sometime during the night, she'd put on her nightgown. She lay on her back, a languorous feeling creeping over her. Dan had gotten up to use the bathroom. Shifting to her side, she cupped her head in her hand, awaiting his return.

Later, she'd wonder what made her turn to look at the door to the hall. There was just enough light in the room for her to see the handle move. Too stunned to speak, she watched the door open slowly.

Frantic, she tried to scream to Dan, but her throat locked. Oh, please, she prayed, be a mistake and go away.

She bit down hard on her lip. Covering her mouth with the sheet, she reached over to the night table, groping for Dan's gun. She held it in her shaking hands, and aimed it squarely at the bandy-legged figure stealing into the room.

Her breath exploded with recognition.

"Freeze!"

Ten

"Stay where you are, Louie."

Louie's eyes were fierce, following the waving gun. He dropped the pipe in his hand. "Lady, I'm harmless." His gaze darted around the room. "Where's Murdock? Ask him."

Never, even in her wildest dreams, had she imagined herself in such a situation. The sweat poured down between her breasts. Her throat refused to function. Her hands were glued to the gun.

And Dan was in the bathroom.

Then she saw the pink teddy bear sitting in the pith helmet. She glared furiously at the crumb who dared intrude on her lovely weekend.

"You make one move before Dan gets in here and I'll blow you to the moon, creep."

"Lady, please put that thing away." Louie, seeing the face of fear in front of him, knew danger. It gave him the bravery to shout. "Murdock, for God's sake, get out here and arrest me! This dame's crazy."

Dan ripped open the bathroom door. "Holy—" In a flash he took stock of the situation. Millie, glassy-eyed and scared out of her wits, was waving the pistol in Louie's direction. It could go off at any time. No wonder he was scared.

"You bastard," he said to Louie. "You're going away for a long, long time for pulling this trick." He eased over to Millie. He didn't want to make any sudden moves.

"Millie darling, give me the gun."

She barely glanced at Dan. "You have the right to remain silent. Anything you say can and will be used against you in a court of law—"

"Geez, Murdock, can't you get that gun?" Sweat ran down Louie's face.

"Honey, those are my lines. Now be a good girl and give me the gun."

She shook her head. No one was going to harm Dan, she told herself. Besides, the metal had grown into her hands.

"Please, lady," Louie said. "Give Murdock the gun."

"Sweetheart." Dan moved closer to her. "I love you. If you shoot this no-good louse, we'll never have all those little Bernards and Bernadettes cluttering up the house."

"That's right, lady. Don't you want them?"

Dan glared at Louie. "Shut up. For your information, this woman shot a bear today. So it would be a cinch for her to take you out. Now—on the floor."

Dan placed his hand over Millie's, prying her fingers loose. "Honey, I love you. Do this for me."

Millie nodded. The gun fell into his hands. Keeping it trained on Louie's prone figure, he helped her sit down on the bed. Then he picked up the phone.

"Ben, I've got a little surprise for you. Can you drive up where we are and pick it up?" He quickly filled Ben in with the situation, then hung up. "Louie, you made one hell of a mistake trying to get me. I'm going to see to it that you rot in jail. Looks like you bought yourself some bad P.R., pal. Even your mob friends won't have anything to do with you when I'm through."

Millie was coming out of her daze. She found herself giving voice to a string of unladylike pronouncements aimed at the intruder on the floor.

She was still fuming when Ben arrived. Her passionate lover was gone; Dan had reverted to being all cop. He had cuffed Louie to the bed and read him his Miranda rights.

After Ben left with Louie, Dan held her in his arms, absorbing the shudders that racked her body. "Darling, you were wonderful." He was back to gentle.

She wiped the tears from her eyes. She was shaking with fear—for him. "He could have hurt you. You were defenseless."

Dan smiled indulgently, making light of the potentially serious situation. "That was a heck of a way to be defenseless."

It wasn't funny. "I want to go home," she said.

He couldn't blame her. The room, the entire

resort, had lost its special flavor now. "All right, darling. We'll dress and leave."

She hadn't heard him, he thought, when he'd said he loved her or when he'd told her he wanted children with her. Sighing, he slipped off the bed. Maybe tomorrow . . .

The next morning Millie caught the first plane out of Tampa to Newark Airport. When she had said she wanted to go home, that's what she'd meant. She had fallen hopelessly in love with Dan. She simply couldn't face the possibility that he could be hurt in the line of duty. If that made her a coward for not wanting to lose a loved one twice, so be it. Dan had been lucky this time. For her the price was too high.

The real estate agent promised to have someone pack her remaining belongings and ship them to New Jersey.

Kipp and his wife Stacy met her at the airport, their faces mirroring their concern when they saw her puffy, red eyes. Wylie had called to tell them what had happened. "You need time, sis," Kipp said. "Dan Murdock sounds like a good man. Don't close the doors behind you."

She refused to talk about it. She refused to spend the night at their house. She wanted to be alone to nurse her wounds. She left her suitcase by the front door while she wandered through her house.

She removed the protective covers from the furniture as she roamed from room to room, imagining the house as it once was, when Frank had been alive. Now it was empty and silent. As empty and silent as she felt.

She'd gone to Florida to run away. She'd left Florida for the same reason.

Sighing, she sat down at the piano in the living room, letting her fingers drift over the keys. She remembered another house and an upright piano, one that wasn't nearly as expensive as her concert grand. Yet it was that house and that piano tugging at her heart. Dan's house and Dan's piano.

He didn't know she was running away. She had told him she needed at least a day to catch up on her work. He'd looked at her quizzically, started to argue, then changed his mind. He'd kissed her hard, telling her everything would be all right. She'd held on to him tightly. "Be careful," she'd said.

"Piece of cake, sweetheart." He'd hurried down the path to his car, excited that Louie was not only behind bars, but he'd be staying there for a very long time.

Once inside her rented home, Millie had called Wylie first, then the airlines. Except for her broken heart, it was hard to picture that she'd been away, things had stayed so much the same in so many ways.

She unpacked her computer. She had work to do. She had promised Wylie she'd have the Dan chapter on her desk within a week.

For four days she followed a strict routine, breaking it only when her back ached so much she had to take a walk. The phone still hadn't been reconnected. She was grateful for that. She needed time to be able to speak calmly with Dan and explain why she'd left.

Assuming he still wanted to talk to her after her running out on him!

He made the national news. Louie's arrest this time was significant because of his newly revealed mob connections. She sat sipping a soda as she watched Dan's interview on the evening news. He answered the questions curtly. It seemed to her it was all he could do to bridle his temper. He hadn't shaved and looked as if he hadn't slept in days. Still, he was beautiful to her.

Oh, my darling, she thought. *Forgive me for adding to your burdens.* If it hadn't been for her, Dan would never have gone to the Ocean Resort. Louie might have stayed away from him and he would never have gotten this sort of publicity. It broke her heart to realize a smart investigative reporter might soon reach into the Murdock past and make the connection Dan clearly feared to make public.

Police Chief Wasach was standing next to Dan. She noticed that Dan tried to hand off the reporters' questions to him. The reporters obviously weren't buying it.

"Were you alone at the time, detective?" one of them asked. "I understand you were in the Ocean Resort's honeymoon suite."

Millie held her breath. Dan looked straight into the camera. He seemed to be sending the message directly to her. "I was with the woman I love and hope to marry . . . if she'll have me."

She gasped with surprise. "Damn you, Murdock. Stop making this harder for me," she exclaimed as the reporters shouted over one another asking questions about this unexpected and colorful new human interest angle to the story.

Over the next three days Millie finished the chapter. Then she called Wylie. "I can't give it to you."

"What?" Wylie's tone clearly announced she'd been afraid of something like this.

Millie's tears came then. She was powerless to stop them. She realized when she finished the chapter that she'd written it for Dan and only for him.

It was the longest love letter she'd ever written. She had sent it express mail to him that morning.

"I've gone back to my earlier material," she told Wylie. "Remember? About the concert pianist who suffered a stroke? I heard him give a concert last year. If you didn't know he was playing with one hand, you'd swear it was with two. I've already polished that piece and put it in the mail. The publisher should be satisfied. It's a good chapter. I'll send you more in a few weeks." She hoped Wylie wouldn't read her the riot act.

"You sure you know what you're doing, Millie?" Wylie didn't mind.

"No, I'm hoping I know what I'm doing. This is one time I could use Ms. M.'s advice."

"Want mine?"

Millie laughed shortly. "Do I have a choice?"

"Go back to him. With all my husbands I've

never felt about a man the way you feel about Dan. You've lost love once. Don't throw it away this time."

The next afternoon Millie stood in her backyard drinking in the beauties of spring. She'd come to a decision about her house, finally. She loved the neighborhood. It was a wonderful area in which to bring up children. She would miss it when she sold it, but it was time to move on. Someone would love this house as she did. But she no longer belonged here.

The gardener had come during her absence, as promised. Bending down, she picked a bouquet of yellow iris. Purple, white, and deep red tulips grew in brilliant clumps, surrounded by grape hyacinth. She loved the spring.

Dan had been on the evening news again the night before. He'd looked marvelous, strong and commanding. When he'd gazed straight into the camera, she could have sworn he was looking at her. She'd turned up the volume, catching every nuance, loving and missing him more than she'd thought possible.

She'd listened with pride as some local politician praised Dan for exposing a major crime syndicate. Dan was given a special commendation. Pete Wasach had smiled broadly as he pinned the medal onto him. She'd chuckled at Dan's expression. His mouth was compressed in a forbidding line.

He hated notoriety or attention. Thanks to her, now he got plenty.

Watching him on television, she had gradually come to terms with her feelings. Nothing was as important as being Dan's wife.

Only she was too late. He hadn't called. He'd
certainly received the chapter by now. Maybe, she
thought, annoyed when the doorbell rang, he'd
change his mind. What man wants to be married to a chicken?

She walked through the house and swung open
the door. A portly, middle-aged man with a bul-
bous nose and watery eyes was standing there.
The sign on his uniform read: *We Deliver Anything.*

"You Ms. M.?" he asked.

"Yes." She couldn't hide her disappointment.
She'd secretly hoped it might be Dan, coming to
tell her he couldn't live without her, and was dragging her back to Florida—by the hair, if necessary.

"This is for you." The man shoved a slim pack-
age at her, then waited.

"Yes, of course," she stammered, realizing the
man wanted his tip. "Wait here." She ran into the
living room for her purse and dug out her Visa
credit card. "I'm sorry. I know this is unorthodox,
but you see, I ran away from someone I met in
Florida. I haven't had time to get to the bank yet
and I've spent all my money on groceries."

He rolled his eyes. "Lady, forget it. You need it
worse than I do." He left, muttering.

Millie fumbled with the wrapping, then stared
at the photograph. She nearly cracked up. It was
Henry and Henrietta. They were begging, their
mouths open.

"He loves me!" she shouted. She dashed to the
phone. Impatiently she counted the rings until
the line was picked up. She almost blurted out
that she wanted to be the mother of all the little

Bernadettes and Bernards they could manage when Ben dryly informed her Dan was away. Another case.

"When will he return?" she asked, crestfallen.

"I'm not sure. All I know is that he said he'll be away until the case is solved. Is there a message? Maybe I can give it to him when he checks in."

"No, never mind. Thanks anyway, Ben." She hung up, feeling glum and miserable. She was still moping when the bell rang again.

"Now what?" She grabbed her credit card, just in case, and yanked open the door.

The young policeman looked very serious and, she thought, nervous. He stood very straight as she stared at him. He coughed, then asked, "Are you Millie Gordon?"

She nodded. Please, she prayed, not bad news about Dan.

The officer stood straighter, if that were possible. His brown eyes were stern. "I have a warrant for your arrest."

She repeated the words soundlessly, unbelieving. "Are you crazy?" she yelled. Thoughts of Dan were wiped from her mind as she stared at the young officer. "I've never done anything wrong in my life. Now please leave me alone. I'm busy."

He squared his shoulders and tugged his cap. "I'm afraid I can't do that. You'll have to come to the station with me to answer the charges."

"What charges?" she asked, frantically trying to remember her lawyer's phone number. This couldn't be happening.

"You'll have to ask that man in the patrol car. He's got the extradition papers."

She pushed him to the side, her glance slicing to the black and white squad car parked in her driveway. The sun's rays prevented her from seeing clearly the face of the man in the backseat, but she'd know the shape of that head anywhere. She had held it to her breast often enough.

"Oh, is that right, officer?" she asked, chuckling.

He cleared his throat again. This was his first arrest. Why, he wondered, did it have to be a gorgeous woman with a glint in her eye that spelled trouble? "Yes, ma'am."

He jumped out of her way as she burst past him, running down the steps as if her life depended on it. He got his wind and took off after her, but he was too late. He groaned as she yanked open the car door and flew onto the lap of the man who sat there grinning.

Grinning! What kind of a crazy arrest was this? He watched closely, just in case he had to give testimony.

Millie flashed her Visa card. "I'm Millie Gordon of the Port Rico Police Department. You'd better come with me, mister. If you don't, your life could be in danger."

"Oh, yeah?" Dan barely got the words out as kisses were rained on his face and neck.

"Yeah." She waved away the policeman, who had poked his head over the front seat.

Dan couldn't wait to get her alone. "In that case, lady," he said solemnly, "I'll do anything you want."

She wrapped her arms around him, kissing him full on the mouth. "Promise?"

He laughed, kissing her back. "Promise. That

doesn't include the mirror on the ceiling, though. My father said I have to make you an honest woman. He's found out no one cares what happened years ago to his brother, my uncle Jack. We'll talk about him later. I love you, Millicent Dolores Gordon, and I want to make me an honest man."

Millie stopped kissing him long enough to get in one last order. She turned to the rookie, who had slid behind the wheel. "City Hall, driver. This man has just been given a life sentence."

Dan stopped nibbling her ear. "What?" he growled. "No time off for good behavior?"

"Not a chance, Murdock," she said, sending him a cocky, self-assured grin. "I'm going to be the best cop's wife you ever saw."

His hand strayed to her thigh. He'd wait until later, until she lay naked in his arms, to tell her she'd have to be the best prosecuting attorney's wife he ever saw.

"Promise?" he asked.

"Your best handcuffs, Murdock."

"What about children? How many do you want?"

"For starters? How about trying for twins? We could make our own team of Bernards and Bernadettes."

Neither paid attention to the gasp coming from the rookie in the other seat.

"That might be fun. What about your job?"

"Ms. M. can work anywhere. Give her a lap computer and she can even work in the maternity ward."

"Not a chance," he said gruffly. "I intend to be in there with you."

"Okay."

He'd never heard her give in so easily. "You're fishing for something. I can tell."

"You bet." She stroked him between his legs.

"Yipes!" he shouted. "Watch it, or we'll be having those twins sooner than you think."

"Driver," Millie commanded, "I said City Hall."

Flabbergasted, Officer Norman Brackman, fresh out of the academy, one week on the force, and taught to show deference to all superiors, even the ones from Florida, asked, "Sir, is this your wish?"

Dan didn't bother to answer. Instead, while the young man shook his head at the antics of the two passengers in his patrol car, Detective Sergeant Daniel J. Murdock of the Port Rico Police Department performed his last official duty.

He lowered Millie onto the seat, shielding her body with his, blocking out the sun, blocking out everything but himself. She was his for keeps.

"In that case, sugar, it's show time. Pucker up."

"Murdock, I thought you'd never ask."

Her throaty laughter wafted into the front seat. It was a sound Officer Brackman wished he'd hear a woman make for him. He started the car, heading for City Hall and the Marriage License Bureau.

After all, he'd had his orders.

THE EDITOR'S CORNER

This coming month brings to mind lions and lambs—not only in terms of the weather, but also in terms of our six delightful LOVESWEPTs. You'll find fierce and feisty, tame and gentle characters in our books next month who add up to a rich and exciting array of folks whose stories of falling in love are enthralling.

First, hold on to your hat as a really hot wind blows through chilly London town in Fayrene Preston's marvelous *The Pearls of Sharah II:* **RAINE'S STORY,** LOVESWEPT #318. When Raine Bennett realized someone was following her through foggy Hyde Park one night, she ran . . . straight into the arms of Michael Carr. He was a stranger who radiated danger and mystery—yet he was a man Raine instinctively knew she could trust. Michael was utterly captivated by her, but the magnificent strand of perfect pearls draped across her exquisite body complicated things. What was she doing with the legendary Pearls of Sharah, which had just been reported stolen to his branch of Interpol? What were her secrets and would she threaten his integrity . . . as well as his heart? This is a dazzling love story you just can't let yourself miss! (Do remember that the Doubleday hardcover edition is available at the same time the paperback is in the stores. Don't miss this chance to collect all three Pearls of Sharah romances in these beautifully bound editions at only $12.95.)

Jan Hudson's **THE RIGHT MOVES,** LOVESWEPT #319, will set your senses ablaze. Jan created two unique characters in her heroine and hero; they were yin and yang, fire and ice, and they could not stay away from each other no matter how hard they tried. Chris Ponder was a spitfire, a dynamo with a temper . . . and with a tow truck. When she took one look at Nick Russo's bedroom eyes, her insides turned to tapioca, and she suddenly wanted to flirt with the danger he represented. But good sense started to prevail. After all, she hardly needed to fall for a handsome charmer who might be all flash and no substance. Still Nick teased, and she felt she might go up in flames . . . especially on one moonlit night that filled her with wonder. This is a breathlessly exciting romance!

In LOVESWEPT #320, **THE SILVER BULLET AFFAIR,** Sandra Chastain shows us once again that love sure can conquer all. When John Garmon learned that his brother Jeffrey's will instructed him to "Take care of Caitlan and the

(continued)

baby—it's mine," he immediately sought out the quicksilver lady who had charmed him at every former meeting. Caitlan proved to be like a fine perfume—good at disappearing and very elusive. She believed that John was her adversary, a villain, perhaps, who might take her baby away if he learned the truth. So how could she lose herself in the hot shivery sensations of his embrace? Bewitched by this fragile woman who broke all the rules, John grows determined to rescue Caitlan from her free-spirited life and the gang of crazy but caring friends who never leave them alone to learn to love each other. A shimmering, vivid love story that we think you'll find a real delight.

The brilliant . . . fun . . . thrilling . . . surprising conclusion to the "Hagen Strikes Again" series, by Kay Hooper, **ACES HIGH**, LOVESWEPT #321, comes your way next month. Skye Prescott was tall, dark, and dangerous, a man who'd never forgotten how Katrina Keller had betrayed him years before. In a world where survival depended on suspicion, he'd fallen in love—and it had broken him as violence never had. When the beautiful redheaded ghost from his past reappeared in his life, Skye was filled with fury, hurt, a desire for revenge—and an aching hunger to make Katrina burn for him again. Katrina had fought her memories, but once she was in his arms, she couldn't fight him or her own primal passion. She was his match, his mate—but belonging to him body and spirit gave him the power to destroy her. When Skye faced his most violent enemy, Trina knew she faced the most desperate gamble of her life. Now, friends, need I tease you with the fact that Hagen also gets his in this fabulous book? I know you've been wondering (as all of us here have) what Kay was going to do for that paunchy devil in terms of a love story. Well, next month you will know. And I can guarantee that Kay has been as delightfully inventive as we had hoped and dreamed she would be.

Please give a great, warm welcome to talented new author Marcia Evanick by getting and enjoying her powerfully emotional romance, **PERFECT MORNING**, LOVESWEPT #322. How this story will touch your heart! When Jason Nesbit entered Riki McCormick's front yard in search of his young daughter, he never expected to find an emerald-eyed vixen as her foster mother. He had just learned that he had a child when his ex-wife died in an accident. Traumatized after her mother's death, the girl had not spoken since. Jason marveled at Riki's houseful of love—and was capti-

(continued)

vated by the sweet, spirited woman who'd made room in her life for so many special children. Under Jason's steamy scrutiny, Riki felt a wave of longing to be kissed breathless and held tight. When his Texas drawl warned her that her waiting days were over, she unpacked her slinkiest lingerie and dreamed of satin sheets and firelight. But courting Riki with seven children around seemed downright impossible. You'll laugh and cry with Jason and Riki as they try to make everyone happy. A keeper!

Halsey Morgan is alive—and Stevie Lee wanted him dead. What a way to open a romance! Glenna McReynolds has created two wonderful, thrilling characters in LOVESWEPT #323, **STEVIE LEE.** Halsey Morgan was Stevie Lee's long-lost neighbor. She had plotted for the last few years to buy his cabin for his back taxes, sell it for a huge profit, and get out of her small town so she could see the world. Handsome Halsey had blazed a trail of adventure from the Himalayas to the Amazon—and was thought to be dead. Now he was back—ruining her plans to escape and melting her with sizzling kisses that almost made her forget why she'd ever wanted to go away. His wildness excited her senses to riot, while his husky voice made her tremble with want. Hal had never stayed anywhere long enough to fall in love, but Stevie was the answer to a loneliness he'd never dared admit. He made her take chances, climb mountains, and taught her how to love him. But could Hal persuade her to risk loving him and follow her dreams while held tight in his arms? Don't miss this great story . . . which, we think you'll agree, knocks your socks off!

Enjoy those blustery days next month curled up with six LOVESWEPTs that are as hot as they are happily-ever-after.

Carolyn Nichols

Carolyn Nichols
Editor
LOVESWEPT
Bantam Books
666 Fifth Avenue
New York, NY 10103